'Our whole lives have been shaken up.

Dad really has bought a bookshop! He didn't even take us with him to check it out first. He went away for the weekend with Rose, and when he came back he said, "Guess what! I've bought a shop."

We just stared at him stunned. He's been acting so crazy. Not like a dad at all. Especially not our dad . . .'

Ruby and Garnett are ten-year-old twins who do *everything* together. But can being a double act work for ever? Especially when everything around them begins to change – beginning with Dad and his new friend, Rose . . .

Double Act is Jacqueline Wilson's seventh title to be published by Corgi Yearling Books. Other titles include *The Suitcase Kid*, which won the 1993 Children's Book Award, and *The Illustrated Mum*, which won the Guardian Children's Fiction Award.

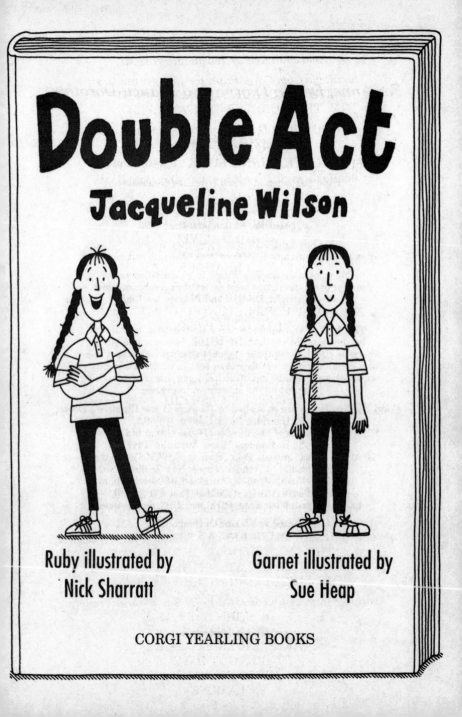

Double Act

Jacqueline Wilson

Ruby illustrated by
Nick Sharratt

Garnet illustrated by
Sue Heap

CORGI YEARLING BOOKS

For Anne, Derek, Thorne and Franca Dorothy

DOUBLE ACT
A CORGI YEARLING BOOK : 0 440 86544 1

First published in Great Britain by Doubleday

PRINTING HISTORY
Doubleday edition published 1995
Corgi Yearling edition published 1996

Corgi Yearling Books are published by Random House Children's Books,
61–63 Uxbridge Road, London W5 5SA,
a division of The Random House Group Ltd,
in Australia by Random House Australia (Pty) Ltd,
20 Alfred Street, Milsons Point, Sydney, NSW 2061, Australia,
in New Zealand by Random House New Zealand Ltd,
18 Poland Road, Glenfield, Auckland 10, New Zealand
and in South Africa by Random House (Pty) Ltd,
Endulini, 5a Jubilee Road, Parktown 2193, South Africa.

Printed and bound in Denmark by
AIT Nørhaven A/S, Viborg

www.**kidsatrandomhouse**.co.uk

ONE

We're twins. I'm Ruby. She's Garnet.

We're identical. There's very few people who can tell us apart. Well, until we start talking. I tend to go on and on. Garnet is much quieter.

That's because I can't get a word in edgeways.

We are exactly the same height and weight. I eat a bit more than Garnet. I love sweets, and I like salty things too. I once ate thirteen packets of crisps in one day. All salt-and-vinegar flavour. I love lots of salt and vinegar on chips too. Chips are my special weakness. I go munch munch munch gulp and they're gone. So then I have to snaffle some of Garnet's. She doesn't mind.

Yes I do.

I don't get fatter because I charge around more. I hate sitting still. Garnet will hunch up over a book for hours, but I get the fidgets. We're both quite good at running, Garnet and me. At our last sports day at school we beat everyone, even the boys. We came first. Well, I did, actually. Garnet came second. But that's not surprising, seeing as I'm the eldest. We're both ten. But I'm twenty minutes older. I was the bossy baby who pushed out first. Garnet came second.

We live with our dad and our gran.

Dad often can't tell us apart in the morning at breakfast, but then his eyes aren't always

open properly. He just swallows black coffee as he shoves on his clothes and then dashes off for his train. Dad works in an office in London and he hates it. He's always tired out when he gets home. But he can tell us apart by then. It's easier in the evening. My plaits are generally coming undone and my T-shirt's probably stained. Garnet stays as neat as a new pin.

That's what our gran says. Gran always used to have pins stuck all down the front of her cardi. We had to be very careful when we hugged her. Sometimes she even had pins sticking out of her mouth. That was when she did her dressmaking. She used to work in this posh Fashion House, pinning and tucking and sewing all day long. Then, after . . .

Well, Gran had to look after us, you see, so she did dressmaking at home. For private customers. Mostly very large ladies who wanted posh frocks. Garnet and I always got the giggles when we peeped at them in their underwear.

Gran made all our clothes too. That was *awful*. It was bad enough Gran being old-fashioned and making us have our hair in plaits. But our clothes made us a laughing stock at school, though some of the mums said we looked a picture.

We had frilly frocks in summer and dinky pleated skirts in winter, and Gran knitted too – angora boleros that made us itch, and matching jumpers and cardis for the cold. Twinsets. And a right silly set of twins we looked too.

But then Gran's arthritis got worse. She'd always had funny fingers and a bad hip and a naughty knee. But soon she got so she'd screw up her face when she got up or sat down, and her fingers swelled sideways and she couldn't make them work.

She can't do her dressmaking now. It's a shame, because she did like doing it so much. But there's one Amazing Advantage. We get to wear shop clothes now. And because Gran can't really make it on the bus into town, we get to *choose*.

Well. Ruby gets to choose.

I choose for both of us. T-shirts. Leggings. Jeans. Matching ones, of course. We still want to look alike. We just want to look normal.

Only I suppose we're not really like the normal sort of family you read about in books. We read a lot of books. Dad is the worst. He keeps on and on buying them — not just new ones, but heaps of old dusty tomes from book

fairs and auctions and Oxfam shops. We've
run out of shelves. We've even run out of floor.
We've got piles and piles of books in every
room and you have to zig-zag around them
carefully or you cause a bookquake. If you
have ever been attacked by fifty or a hundred
very hard hardbacks then you'll know this is
to be avoided at all costs. There are big boxes

of books upstairs too that Dad hasn't even
properly sorted. Sometimes you have to climb
right over them to get somewhere vital like
the toilet.

Gran keeps moaning that the floorboards won't stand up to all that weight. They do tend to creak a bit. Dad gets fussed then and agrees it's ridiculous and sometimes when we're a bit strapped for cash he loads a few boxes into our old car and takes them to a second-hand bookshop to sell. He does sell them too – but he nearly always comes back with another lot of bargains, books he couldn't possibly resist.

Then Gran has another fierce nag and Dad goes all shifty, but when he brings her a big carrier of blockbuster romances from a boot fair she softens up considerably. Gran likes to sit in her special chair with lots of plumped-up cushions at her back, her little legs propped up on her pouffe, a box of Cadbury's Milk Tray wedged in beside her, and a juicy love story in her lap. They're sometimes very *rude*, and when Garnet and I read over her shoulder she swats us away, saying we'll find out something we shouldn't. Ho ho. We found it all out *ages* ago.

Dad reads great fat books too, but they're not modern, they're all classics – Charles Dickens and Thomas Hardy. If we have a look at Dad's book we wonder what the Dickens they're on about and they seem *very* Hardy, but Dad likes them. He also likes boys' adventure books – really old ones where the boys wear knickerbockers and talk like twits: 'I say, old bean', and 'Truly spiffing', and 'Tophole'.

Garnet likes old books too – stuff like *Little Women* and *What Katy Did* and all those E. Nesbit books. And she reads twin books too. Books like *The Twins at St Clare's*. And all the *Sweet Valley Twins*. I read them too, because you can read them nice and quickly. But the books *I* like best are true stories about flashy famous people. Actors and actresses. I skip everything boring and just read the best bits when they're on telly and making movies and all over the front of the newspapers, very flashy and very famous.

We're going to be famous too someday, you bet. So I've started writing our life-story already. It's funny, Garnet is usually the one who writes stuff. Her writing's neater than mine. So often I get her to do my schoolwork. She doesn't mind.

Yes I do.

I was rifling through one of the boxes of books upstairs and right at the bottom there was this lovely fat red book. Ruby red, with a leather spine and one word picked out in gold lettering: ACCOUNTS.

I thought it was the title but when I opened it up there were just all these blank pages.

I asked Dad what had happened to the story and he said it wasn't a proper book at all. Accounts are sums. You add up everything you've bought. That's keeping accounts.

'Only I don't like keeping accounts. I just feel guilty seeing how much I've spent,' said Dad. 'You can have it to scribble in, twins.'

So I'm scribbling away.

I'm not.

Yes you are. I keep letting you have a turn. And I'm not just writing about me, I'm writing about us. Giving an account of ourselves. Hey, Garnet, find a dictionary and look up the word 'account'.

Account: 1. A verbal or written report, description, or narration of some occurrence, event, etcetera.

Yeah! That's exactly what I'm doing. Writing an account of our lives.

Everything's a bit boring right this minute but maybe soon we'll somehow get our big chance and we'll achieve our lifetime's ambition and be actresses.

I don't want to be an actress.

Of course we want to be actresses. Honestly, Garnet, give over jogging me. (She can be a bit stupid and shy at times. She doesn't think we'll ever make it as flashy film stars, but I keep telling her all we need is CONFIDENCE. She keeps going on at me now, saying she doesn't want to be a star. Well, that's mad. She can't mean it. Who on earth wouldn't want to show off all day in front of the camera and go to posh parties every night with all the other stars?)

We'll live in our own flash flat with masses

of flowers in every room and huge boxes of chocs to dip into whenever we fancy, and we'll wear ruby-red sequin frocks and ruby jewellery to match – OK OK, Garnet, you can have garnets, only they're not as precious and valuable and sparkly, *are* they?

That's not what you wanted to say? Well, what *do* you want to say then? All right. You write your bit now. Go on. Here you are. Get cracking. You write about you.

I don't know what to put.

I'm not used to writing about me. It's always us. I do like writing though. I was a bit annoyed when Ruby bagged this beautiful red book and started scribbling all that stuff. I thought we could maybe use it to write down our plays. We've always played these pretend games together right from when we were little. We pretend to be other people and make things up. It used to seem so real that it would get muddled into our ordinary life. It can still seem real for me, but Ruby often mucks about and won't play properly. She doesn't like going over and over a play, she just wants me to keep making up new ones for us. She doesn't seem to realize it's hard work. And if we keep starting on new plays then some of the best old plays get forgotten. I want to write them down properly to keep them safe.

I like making up plays and I don't mind acting them out when it's just Ruby and me and we're totally private and imagining it so it could almost be actually happening, but I can't bear proper acting.

Ruby and I were twin sheep in the nativity play when we were still in the Infants and it was one of the most truly awful experiences of my life.

Not the most awful, of course.

That was when

Look, you're not writing any of that sad stuff, I won't let you. This is me again. Ruby. Garnet's just gone off, all humpy because I happened to scratch her a tiny little bit when I snatched the pen. I asked her nicely first. And it's my turn now. You have to be able to take turns fairly when you're twins.

That stuff she wrote is daft anyway. What's the point of writing plays down in books? You should *play* plays. And she's got to be an actress because that's what we've always wanted to be, and while we're still trying to get famous we can do adverts and game shows on the telly. Identical twins are a Mega-Novelty.

Garnet can't reject Fame just because of

that one unfortunate experience being a
sheep when we were little.

   She got so worked up and nervous when we
had to perform that she wet herself. On stage.
In front of everyone. But it didn't really
matter. I don't know why she still gets all hot
and bothered if I happen to bring it up. It was
dead appropriate, actually, because that's
what real sheep do all the time. They don't
hang around the stable with their back legs
crossed, holding it in. They go all over the
place. Which is what Garnet did. And
everyone thought it was ever so funny. Except
Garnet.
   Got to go now. I can smell Sunday dinner.
Yorkshire pud, yummy yummy yummy in my
tummy.

Ruby! You mean pig. You've put about me being the sheep!

Look, *you* were the one who mentioned it first. You went on and on about it.

Yes, but I didn't say what happened. It was my most painful and humiliating secret. And now you've told, Ruby.

I haven't *told*. I've written. And this accounts book is secret. Just for us. We can write everything down in it. All our secrets.

Yes, but you haven't written down your secrets. You've written down mine.

Oh, quit fussing. Let's go and eat. I'm starving.

Gran's a bit cross because Dad's ever so late back from his car-boot sale and she's had the dinner turned down low for the last half-hour and her Yorkshire is going all sad and soggy.

Like some silly twin. Come on, Gran's calling.

Dad should have been back ages ago. He is

all right, isn't he?

Of course he is. You are an old worryguts, Garnet. He'll have just bought up an entire bookstall, that's all, and he'll be having trouble stuffing them all into the car. You know what he's like.

Yes, but he's not usually as late as this. And he likes Gran's Sunday dinners as much as we do. What if he's had an accident?

Oh, Garnet, shut up. Coming, Gran.

TWO

We haven't been able to write a proper
account because tons and tons of stuff has
been happening. And now I suppose I should
write it all out and yet I don't know where to
start. You have a go, Garnet. Go on.

*I don't want to go on. I want to stop. No. I
want to go backwards. Back past the day Dad
was late back from the boot fair. Back past the
ordinary us twins and Dad and Granny day
after day part. Back through the awful bit
when Mum died and*

STOP IT STOP IT STOP IT

No, Ruby. We can't stop now. We've got to remember. And don't you see? We've got to make Dad remember. And then he'll stop seeing Rose.

Ah. All right. But tell it quickly. The bit about Mum. Tell it as if it was a story and not real so that it won't hurt so much.

Once upon a time a man called Richard fell in love with a girl called Opal. Opals are beautiful stones that shine all different colours. But some say opals are unlucky. This girl Opal was beautiful and she shone and Richard knew he was lucky lucky lucky to have met her.

Richard loved Opal. He sometimes mucked about and called her Oh Pal. Because he said she was his pal. And he gave her an opal ring.

Where's that ring? Remember how we used to be allowed to try it on? But I haven't seen it for ages. Oh no. Oh Garnet, you don't suppose Dad will give it to *Rose*?

No! Of course not. Gran's got it safe in her jewel box and she says we'll get it when we're grown up.

Which one of us? It ought really to be me, seeing as I'm the eldest. But I'll let you borrow it sometimes. If you're careful.

I'm the careful one. Look, you've interrupted my story now.

Go on then. You got to the ring bit. Dad gave Mum the ring.

Richard gave Opal a beautiful opal ring, milky-white but with all different pinks and blues and greens and purples, sparkling like magic whenever it caught the light.

They got their own flat.

They got married.

They had twin daughters.

Which is which? I'm that one, the baby with Mum.

No, that's me. You're the baby with Dad. I drew it so I should know.

Well, I can't help that. The baby with Mum is the biggest baby, you just look and see. And *I* was the biggest, we both know that. That's baby Ruby. I'll show you.

It doesn't matter anyway. OK, you're the baby with Mum.

Right. Well. Mum held you too, of course. She held me and then she held you and Dad held me and then

And then we grew up a bit and we could toddle around and we didn't need to be held. Though we still had cuddles with Mum. We sat on her lap. Both of us together. I can remember.

You're just remembering that photograph. Hey, let's stick it in the accounts book.

It's not just the photo. I can remember. She felt so soft and yet her arms could hold you so

21

*tight you felt safe. And there was her flowery
smell, and her curly hair tickled. She tickled
us too, remember? Round and round the
garden and then she'd tickle us under our
arms and we'd go all squirmy. Remember
that, Ruby?*

*(She's gone all quiet. She can't stand
remembering because it makes her so sad and
she can't ever stand being unhappy. She won't
ever cry. That's one of the few ways people tell*

us apart. If one of us has gone all red and watery-eyed then it's me.

I think I might cry a bit when I write this next part. I'll go back to doing it like a story. And I'll scribble it down ever so quickly.)

The twins started school, and Opal and Richard went to work and at the weekend they did fun things like going swimming and shopping and they had days at the seaside. All the normal nice family things. But then everything stopped being normal and nice. Opal got a bit sick. Then she had to go into hospital. She was all right for a bit after that. But then she got sick again. She couldn't work any more. She lay on the sofa at home. Gran had to meet the twins from school. Richard stopped working and looked after Opal. But she couldn't get better. She died. So they stopped being a family.

There. I've written it. Do you want to read what I put, Ruby? No, she doesn't. It was three years ago. When we were seven. But we're ten now and it's all right again. We can't ever be our old family but we're a new family now. Gran lives with us and she's not like a mother, but then no-one can ever be like a mother to us. NO-ONE. NO-ONE AT ALL. ESPECIALLY NOT STUPID FRIZZY DIZZY ROSE.

This is Rose.

No, THIS is Rose.

Yes, that's Rose. Only she's even worse than that. What does Dad see in her? He's the only one that likes her. Gran doesn't like her one little bit.

Gran's face when Dad turned up with Rose that Sunday! We all just stared at her. And Dad came out with all this guff about how she'd helped him when his bag of books broke, and then surprise surprise her car wouldn't start so he'd given her a lift and they'd popped into a pub for a quick drink on the way home and she was all set to have a sandwich for her lunch and Dad said he'd got a proper roast-beef-and-Yorkshire job cooking for him at home and she went Oooh it's ages since I had a proper Sunday dinner like that so guess what, folks. He brought her back. To share our Sunday lunch.

'There's no problem, is there, Gran?' Dad said.

'No, of course not. Do come and sit down at the table, Rose. There's plenty of food. I'm afraid the beef will be a bit overdone and I can't take pride in my Yorkshire today. It *was* lovely and light and fluffy, but . . .'

'But I waylaid your son-in-law and kept him down the pub and mucked up your meal,' said Rose, and she actually laughed. 'Sorry about that,' she said, though she didn't look the *slightest* bit sorry.

Gran had to smile back at her through gritted teeth like it was funny.

We didn't smile though, did we, Garnet?

She couldn't take the hint though. She chatted away to us, nattering on about telly programmes and pop records and stuff, as if she'd known us years and years. And she kept trying to remember which of us was which.

'Now, you're Garnet, right?' she said to me. 'And you're Ruby,' she said to Garnet.

'Yes,' we said. 'Right.'

'Wrong,' said Dad, laughing uneasily. 'That's Ruby. And that's Garnet. They're a pair of jokers. Even Gran and I get confused at times.'

'Speak for yourself,' Gran said huffily. 'I'm sorry the beef was so dry. Though it would have been just cooked through a treat an hour or so ago. Anyway. Apple pie and cream? Help me clear the plates, girls.'

We helped her clear and when we came

back with the pudding plates I sat in Garnet's chair and she sat in mine. Rose was none the wiser. She nattered away to me, calling me Garnet, and she jabbered stuff to Garnet, calling her Ruby.

'Yes, I'm beginning to be able to tell you apart,' she said. 'You're Ruby. And you're Garnet. Yes. Right.'

'Well. Not *quite* right,' said Dad. He came out with this false ho-ho-ho as if it was a great joke. 'Stop teasing poor Rose, twins. I'm afraid they've swopped seats. They're always doing it. I'd just call each girl "Twin" and be done with it, Rose.'

'Oh, I think that's awful,' said Rose. 'I couldn't stand that if I were a twin.'

Well, certainly twin Roses would be AWFUL.

'You're two separate people who just happen to be sisters, aren't you, Garnet and Ruby. Or Ruby and Garnet. Whichever. I've got muddled.'

'We like being called Twin,' I told her.

'That's what they call us at school,' said Garnet.

'We *are* twins . . .' I said.

'So we like . . .' said Garnet.

'Being called . . .' I said.

'Twins,' we said simultaneously.

27

Rose raised one eyebrow and gave a little nod.

'OK OK,' she said. 'Got it.'

She stopped trying to be so matey with us then. She tried complimenting Gran on her apple pie but Gran stayed as dried up as the dinner and barely said a word. So Dad did all the talking, on and on, saying all this silly stuff and pulling faces and telling stupid stories.

He didn't sound like Dad at all.

It was as if *he'd* swopped with a new twin dad.

He didn't go back to being our dad even when we'd got rid of Rose at last.

'Well, what did you think of her?' he asked eagerly.

I looked at Garnet. She looked at me. I raised one eyebrow. She raised one too. Then we both turned sideways and pretended to be sick.

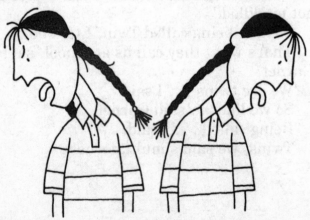

'All right, all right. You've done enough clowning around for one day,' Dad said crossly.

'Yes, don't be so rude, Ruby and Garnet,' said Gran – but she didn't sound a bit cross.

'Did you like Rose, Gran?' Dad asked.

'Well. She seems nice enough. I suppose. A bit . . . pushy, inviting herself to lunch like that.'

'No, I invited her,' said Dad. 'I didn't think you'd make such a big deal about it, actually. You've always said you wished I'd socialize a bit more, bring a few friends home, not stay so wrapped up in the past.'

'Yes, dear. And I mean that. I'm only too pleased that you want to bring people back. Though if you could have just phoned to give me a bit of warning . . . And you do want to go a bit carefully with that type of woman.'

'What do you mean, *type*?' said Dad, really angry now.

'Now, Richard, don't get in such a silly state,' said Gran, as if he was our age. 'It's just that she seems a bit eager. She's never set eyes on you before today and yet she's all over you, even trying to act like one of the family.'

'I've known Rose for months, if you must know,' said Dad. 'She's got her own bric-a-brac stall in the arcade – we're forever bumping into each other at boot fairs. I've always wanted to get to know her better, she's so bubbly and warm and friendly. I don't know how you can talk about her like that – she's a lovely girl.'

'Girl!' said Gran. 'She'll never see thirty again.'

'Well, neither will I,' Dad shouted. 'And it's about time I started making the most of my life, OK?'

He stormed off out of the house, slamming the door. There was a horrible silence after he'd left. Garnet got hold of my hand and squeezed it tight. She looked like she was going to cry. *Gran* looked like she was going to cry too.

We were all shocked by the row. We don't ever have rows in our family.

It's all that Rose's fault.

Yes, it's all Rose's fault. She started all the changes. She comes every Sunday now. And in the week sometimes. And Dad goes out with her in the evenings and when they come back in the car, they KISS.

THREE

I hate changes. I want every day to be the same. I've always been like it, even before Mum died.

I couldn't stand our first day at school.

Everybody stared at us because we were different. And the whole day was different. We couldn't play our own games and talk in our

*own private language. It felt like we couldn't
even be twins, because the teacher sat me on
one side of the classroom and Ruby on the
other. She said it was so she could tell us
apart.*

*I felt as if she'd somehow torn us apart. I
didn't feel a whole person at all. I felt like a
half, as if an arm and a leg and most of my
head were the other side of the room stuck to
Ruby. I didn't know how to think without her.*

Well, naturally. I'm the oldest. I'm the
DOMINANT twin. That's what they call the
one that's born first. That's me. I'm the Big
Cheese. You're just the Little Crumb.

*You didn't like us being separated either,
Ruby. You didn't cry*

You did.

*but you were ever so naughty and so we got
sent to the headteacher and she said, 'Why are
you so unhappy, Garnet? Why are you so
naughty, Ruby?' and we said, 'We want to sit
together.' And she said, 'Is that all? Simple!'*

*And it was simple. We sat together. I didn't
cry any more. And Ruby wasn't naughty. Well,
she was, but not so much.*

*But it still took me ages and ages to get
used to school. But now it's OK. Everyone's so
used to us they don't stare. We're just The
Twins. That's the way we want it. We sit
together in every lesson. We're always
partners. We sit next to each other at lunch.
We even go to the loo together.*

*We're good at lessons. We sometimes come
top, especially when we have to write stories or
do a project.*

But we like Drama best. We're absolutely fabulous at Drama. Well. *I* am. Garnet goes all red and gets her words mixed up.

Don't start, Ruby.

Well, you do. Only you wouldn't if you'd stop being so shy. I don't know why you're so shy. *I* never feel shy.

Look, I just want to write about

You've been writing for ages and ages and you keep waffling on about us back in the Infants and who's bothered about baby stuff like that? Write about what's happening now. All the horrible bit.

Well, give me the pen.

Say please then. Hey! Get off!
'Are you two girls having a fight?'
That's Gran. She's seen us snatching the pen from each other.
'You can share nicely if you try. Now you're going to have to remember all I've taught you when you go. *She's* not the type to bother with good manners.'
'Oh,Gran. I don't want to go!' I said, and I

flung myself on to her lap.

'Watch my hip! And my knee! Ruby, you great lump, get off of me,' said Gran – but she cuddled me close all the same.

'Can I come and join in the cuddle too?' I asked.

I sat on the arm of the chair so I didn't hurt Gran's other hip and knee, but she reached out and pulled me properly on to her lap.

We clung tight. I started crying.

'Stop it, Garnet,' said Ruby, and she pinched me hard. Her face was all screwed up. She was scared I'd make her start crying, even though she never cries. Gran's eyes were all watery too.

'Dear oh dear,' she said, sniffling. She patted us with her poor hands, the fingers all slipping sideways with arthritis. She fumbled up the sleeve of her cardi for her hankie and mopped my face and hers, and then pretended to blow Ruby's nose.

'We'd better turn off the waterworks. I don't want a puddle in my chair,' said Gran.

'Oh Gran, please please please come with us,' Ruby begged.

'Now don't you start, young Ruby. You know it's all settled and decided.'

'But we'll miss you so, Gran!' I said, nuzzling into her warm woollen chest.

'And I'll miss both of you, my girls. But you can come and stay with me on visits – you can sleep either end of the sofa and bring your sleeping bags – and I'll maybe come to this new place for Christmas.'

'Not maybe. You've GOT to come.'

'We'll see. Of course, there's probably no point. She doesn't have a clue about cooking. She probably won't even bother to have a proper turkey.'

'So why can't we all come to you for Christmas, Gran, and then we can have Christmas dinner the way you do it, with cranberry sauce and little chipolatas and chestnut stuffing, yummy yummy,' said Ruby.

'That oven in my new flat is so small it would be hard put to cook a chicken in it,' said Gran. 'Sorry, pet. No more Christmas dinners.'

'No more roast potatoes with special crispy bits and Christmas pud with little silver charms and traffic-light jelly, red and yellow and green,' Ruby wailed.

'I think you're going to miss my cooking more than you'll miss me,' said Gran, shaking her head. 'Come on now, you're both squashing me something chronic. You'd better get back to your writing. Is it something for school?'

There's no point doing anything for school. Because we won't be going there much longer. We've got to go to a new school. In a new place. In a new life. And we're going to hate it.

It's all her fault. We hate her. WE HATE HER.

Yes. We hate her. It all started when Dad met Rose. She kept coming round upsetting us. Barging in. Changing things.

She changed Dad. It isn't just the way he acts, all loopy and lovey-dovey, yuck yuck yuck. She's changed his clothes. He always used to wear just ordinary Dad clothes. Jumpers. Trousers. Suits and white shirts on weekdays, with stripy ties. She started with the ties. She bought him this bright red flowery number.

Then it was Marilyn Monroe. And Mickey Mouse. Dad looked a bit of a cartoon himself in all these daft ties. She didn't stop there. Oh no.

Would you believe, Donald Duck underpants!

At least they were hidden under his trousers. She started on his shirts next. Green stripes. Red check. Blue polka dot.

She said they brightened up his dull old suit.

She was worse with his weekend clothes. She made him give his tracksuit and his comfy old cords to Oxfam. She said they were old man's clothes. She's turned Dad into a new man. A new stupid trendy twit of a dad

in black jeans and
denim jackets and
lumberjack shirts.

She even calls him a new name. Rick. It's
Rick this, Rick that. Sometimes it's even
Ricky. It doesn't half make you feel Sicky.

Gran can't bear it either.

'His name's *Richard*,' she hissed one day.
'We've always called him Richard. No-one
ever calls him Ricky or Rick.'

She said it in the sort of voice that makes
Garnet squirm. But Rose isn't the squirmy
sort. She just smiled.

'*I* call him Rick,' she said.

Gran scowled and sucked her teeth.

'Oh dear,' said Rose sympathetically. 'Is the
pain really bad today?'

Rose is the Pain.

But Gran is in pain too. Her arthritis has got horrid. Sometimes she can't even get out of bed and Ruby and I have to help her. And it takes her ages and ages to get down the stairs with her hip. And up the stairs to the loo. And when she's in her chair she gets stuck and we have to heave, Ruby one side, me the other.

How is she going to manage without us helping her?

She's moving to sheltered housing. We thought that meant she was being housed in a bus shelter.

It's not as bad as that. It's a little flat on the ground floor and she's going to have a Home Help and an Alarm Button.

I feel as if I have an Alarm Button inside me and it's going off all the time.

We're moving too. Garnet and me. And
Dad. And *Her*. Dad lost his job. It's called
Being Made Redundant. Dad said he didn't
care. He'd always hated that boring old office.
But he looked a bit shocked all the same.

'So how are you going to manage without
your boring old salary?' said Gran, sniffing.
'Oh, Richard, you're such a fool. How could
you spoil all your chances like this? And
you've got the twins to think of, too.'

'It wasn't my fault,' he said.

'You've never shown the right attitude. And
since you've taken up with that Rose, you've
turned into . . . into a *hippy*.'

'Oh, for goodness sake—'

'Those silly ties and shirts were the last
straw. Of course they got rid of you. So what
are you going to do now? Have you looked at
the Jobs Vacant in the papers?'

'I don't want that sort of job any more,' said
Dad. 'I've been thinking. They're giving me
quite a bit of cash as my redundancy pay. It's
my chance for a whole new start. We could
sell up here, get a little shop in the country
somewhere. A bookshop. You've always been
on and on at me to sell some of my books!'

'You're talking nonsense,' said Gran. 'Well,
count me out.'

Count us out too, Dad! Garnet and me. We

don't want to be part of any of this.

We don't want to move to a silly old shop in the country! We don't want to leave Gran. We don't want to leave all our friends. We don't want to leave our school. We don't want to leave our old lives. We don't want to live with you. Not if it means we've got to live with *her*. Because she's coming too. Rose.

We wish she'd get greenfly and mildew and wilt.

FOUR

If our writing's a bit shaky, it's because we're
doing this account in the van.

We feel shaky. Our whole lives have been
shaken up.

Dad really has bought a bookshop! He
didn't even take us with him to check it out
first. He went away for the weekend with
Rose, and when he came back he said, 'Guess
what! I've bought a shop.'

We just stared at him, stunned. He's been
acting so crazy. Not like a dad at all.
Especially not our dad.

We're used to him saying, 'Guess what! I've
bought another box of books.'

But you don't buy a book*shop* just like that.
You're meant to hang around for months,
getting it surveyed and seeing solicitors.

'It's all simple,' said Dad. 'This sweet old
couple are retiring and are happy to move out
straightaway. If I can't sell our own house, I'll
let it out to students for a bit. Your gran's got
her sheltered flat all worked out. Rose only
rents her room, and she can shut up her stall
in the arcade any time, so she hasn't got any
problems either.'

We're the ones with the problems. Garnet
and me.

We don't even get considered.

'Why didn't you take us with you to see if
we like it?' I said.

'You'll love it,' said Dad. 'The village is right
out in the country, beside a river, with hills
all around. It's a real story-book place.
There's a pond with puddleducks straight out
of Beatrix Potter. There's just this one street
of shops. Ours is in the middle. We'll fit it out
with shelves and Rose can have the window
for her bric-a-brac. She's got all sorts of ideas

44

for getting it done up. And there's plenty of room upstairs. You two can have the attic for your bedroom – you'll like that.'

Sarah Crewe gets stuck in an attic in A Little Princess *and she has to act like a servant to all the girls in her school. Though at least she got to stay in her school.*

We've had to leave our school.
It was awful saying goodbye.

But it was much worse saying goodbye to

Ruby doesn't want to write it. She always leaves the worst bit to me. I don't want to write it either.

45

*Oh, Gran. We do miss you. We miss you ever
so ever so much. You used to get cross and you
were strict and sometimes you even smacked,
but you didn't hurt because of your poor
hands and you couldn't help being strict
because you're old and you were only cross
when we were naughty.*

*But we do so wish you were with us now.
You could be cross and strict and smack all
the time and we wouldn't mind a bit.*

*You didn't get cross and strict and smack
when we took you to your new flat. But you
weren't all happy and smiley. You looked so
small and scrunched up and sad and it was
so awful.*

*We helped you put your chair and your
china cabinet and all the rest of your stuff in
your new room, but they didn't look right.
They didn't look yours. It didn't look like a
home.*

*This funny old man next door came round
to say hello and he gave you a bunch of
flowers he'd grown in his garden. Dad teased
you and said you'd got yourself a boyfriend
already, but you wouldn't smile. And when
Dad said he hoped you'd be really happy in
your new flat and he was sure it was all for
the best, you just sniffed. You didn't say
anything, but you looked at Dad and it was as*

if you were shrieking: Who are you kidding?

You didn't even kiss Dad properly goodbye,
just gave him your cheek. And we don't blame
you either, Gran.
    You kissed us. And we kissed you. Lots and
lots.

We didn't talk to Dad either. We're still not speaking to him properly. Or Rose. We don't need to. We can just speak to each other. In Twinspeak, so they can't understand.

Garnet and I have this special language. We've got heaps of made-up words for things. Sometimes we don't use words at all, we use signs. Little tiny things like widening our eyes or putting our heads slightly to one side. We signal to each other and then both start up a pretend coughing fit or sneeze simultaneously or shriek with manic laughter.

Rose isn't used to this. It doesn't half make her jump.

'Pack it in,' says Dad.

I glance at Garnet.

'Pack it in what, Dad?' we say simultaneously.

'Less of the cheek,' says Dad, taking one hand off the steering wheel and swatting at us.

'How do they *do* that?' Rose asks.

'How do we do what?' we say.

'Stop it! You're giving me the creeps. Can you really read each other's thoughts?' she says, shivering.

'Of course they can't,' says Dad.

'Then how can they say the same thing at the same time in that weird way?' Rose says, peering at us.

'I don't know,' says Dad, shrugging.

'*We* know,' we say, and we raise our eyebrows and make our eyes glitter in a mysterious and mystic manner.

We wait until Rose turns round again and starts fiddling with the old van radio, trying to tune it to a station. I point to it and nudge Garnet. We both start singing loudly, our timing spot on.

Rose gasps.

'Cut it out, twins,' says Dad sharply.

I turn my fingers into pretend scissors and

make lots of cutting movements. Garnet does the same.

'Oh, very funny,' says Dad, not at all amused.

When he's concentrating on the road, I change the scissors to a dagger and mime a sudden bloody attack on Rose. Garnet does likewise, only she's not quite quick enough. Dad sees, so Garnet shakes her arm quickly, making out she's got cramp.

'What are you playing at, you two?' says Dad.

We blink at him and shrug.

Dad sighs with exasperation, and then takes one hand off the steering wheel and puts his arm round Rose.

I nudge Garnet and we both make a very rude noise.

Dad's hand tightens on Rose's shoulder, but he doesn't say anything. She doesn't say anything either. Neither do we. The radio keeps buzzing and fading and going funny.

I feel a bit like that too. Maybe I'm starting to feel car-sick. Well, van-sick. Ooh good, if I'm going to throw up then I shall aim at Rose.

Ruby was sick. She managed to hit Rose. And me.

Only little splashes on you.

You're not supposed to be writing, in case you get sick again.

I did great, didn't I?

Yes, but I'd sooner you didn't do it again. Rose got through a whole box of tissues, mopping away. Dad had to stop at the next service station and we had to go to the Ladies. I washed and Ruby washed. Rose positively scrubbed and changed her sweater and jeans, scrunching the stained smelly stuff into a plastic bag.
'I think you two belong in the bag too,' she said, sighing. 'Look, I don't care if you act like idiots, but it isn't half upsetting your dad.'

*We didn't say anything. But Ruby smiled,
even though she was still sick and shivery.*

*'Don't you want your dad to be happy?' said
Rose, looking at Ruby and then at me.*

Not with you!

*'He's had a really tough time the last few
years. You two were only tiny so you probably
didn't realize, but he nearly went to pieces
after your mum died.'*

*We stared at her silently, hating her. How
dare she! We felt like we were in little pieces
too.*

*'It was really tough for him, but he kept on
going for your sake. He did his best to get on
with your gran, even though she can be so
difficult at times.'*

How does she have the nerve *to criticize our
gran!*

*'He didn't have any fun, he never went out
anywhere, he was so lonely,' she said.*

*How could he possibly have been lonely? He
had us!*

*'He kept slaving away at that boring old job
in the city, even though it nearly drove him
crazy. He was like this old old man even
though he's barely thirty.'*

She's mad. He's our dad. He is old.

*'But now he's got this big chance. A whole
new life. Something that he's always wanted.*

And he's been like a little kid – so excited. But you two are spoiling it all. Can't you see that?'

Yes, we can see it. That's what we want. It's not us that's spoiling anything. She's got it all wrong. It's her. It's her it's her it's her.

FIVE

We're here. And we hate it.

Yes. We hate it.

It's the worst place in the whole world, and
we're stuck here with the worst people. Stuck
stuck stuck.

Well, the place itself *isn't that bad.*

Yes it is!

No, wait, Ruby. I don't mean the shop. Or the village. But the countryside itself is OK, isn't it? Especially the hills. I hated going for a walk with Rose and Dad, but when we were up in the hills and we saw all the sheep and the wild ponies and we got right to the top and we were almost up in the sky and we could see for miles and it felt like we could just step off the edge and fly—

Will you put a sock in it, Miss Arty-Farty Show-Off. All this sky-and-fly stuff! You sound like you're writing a poem for school. 'My-day-in-the-country'. Boring! And the country's boring too. Grey hills and grey fields and grey trees and grey rain.

Rose doesn't think much of it either. She's still all smarmy with Dad, but we're wearing her down – and this certainly isn't her dream place to live. She got seriously fed up when I accidentally on purpose waved that branch near the washing line and snagged all her stupid tights and the village shop only sells

pale beige old-lady tights. Old Rose could have sold her soul for a Sock Shop then.

She hates the Superstore too. Because it doesn't have any decent fruit or veg and the bread's sliced up in bags.

Yes, but Dad says he'll grow raspberries and tomatoes and runner beans in the back garden and he's going to have a go at making our own bread.

Do me a favour, Garnet! Dad can't even make *toast*. Gran was always going on about how hopeless he was.

Dad says that was because she never let him try his hand at anything. She always said, 'Come on now, out from under my feet, stop cluttering up my kitchen.' Oh dear. We do miss Gran so. We wish she was here.

No, we wish *we* were *there*. Instead of here in this hateful dump. We don't fit in.

Dad's shop doesn't fit in either. Especially now. The antique shops are all painted white or cream or very pale beige. Dad's shop started off dirty white too, so he decided to brighten it up a bit.

'I'm going to call it The Red Bookshop,' he

said. 'Because of my three girls. Rubies are red, Garnets are red, and Roses are red. So let's go the whole hog and paint it red too.'

He motored miles and miles to the nearest Do-it-Yourself Store in Hineford and came back with pots of stinging scarlet paint. We were supposed to help Rose wash the front of the shop and rub the peeling paint, but after about ten minutes scrubbing and sloshing, Ruby threw her sponge in the bucket and said, 'We're fed up with this lark,' and sauntered off.

So I threw my sponge in the bucket too, and sidled after my sister.

'Hey, come back, you lazy beasts,' Rose shouted, and she threw a sponge at us.

It glanced off Ruby, still sopping wet. Ruby took hold of it and aimed. She's a very good aimer. It caught Rose full in the face.

We ran right away then. We walked round and round the village and up and down the stream and then we went down by the river but it was too muddy and we weren't wearing our wellies and I slipped and got mud all over my bottom. It looked AWFUL. And Ruby made it worse because she kept laughing at me. I tried to rub the mud off with grass but it was useless.

I started to cry and Ruby got cross.

'Why do you always have to be such a baby?' she said. 'Look, it's your own fault for slipping like that. And it doesn't matter anyway – they're only your old jeans. And she can't tell us off because she's not our mother or any part of our family. So stop snivelling.'

'I can't go back through the village like this. People will look at me and laugh.'

'No they won't. They won't even notice, honest,' said Ruby.

She wasn't being honest. They did notice. This crowd of children fishing by the bridge saw us and stared. First of all because we were strangers. Second because we're twins. But then they saw the muck all over my jeans and then they really stared. And sniggered. And shouted horrible rude suggestions.

Ruby caught hold of me by the wrist and gave me a little shake to stop me crying again.

She marched us straight up to them instead of
skulking away, like I wanted. Her face was as
red as her name.

'What's so funny?' she said, when we were
right up close to them. She made me say it too.
'What's so funny?' we said in unison.

They were mostly around our age, but some
were bigger. Ruby didn't care.

Some of the littler kids stepped backwards.
They weren't just worried about Ruby. It was
me too. Because we were walking in step and
talking exactly together and when we do that
lots of people find it really spooky.

The bigger boys weren't easily fazed though.
One fat one with silly sideways hair said
something ever so rude and horrible and they
all laughed again.

'Ooh! Being covered in mud is funny, is it?'
said Ruby.

'Funny, is it?' we said together.

Then Ruby looked at me and looked at the muddy grass and I knew what she was going to do. I knew I had to do it too. We bent, we sunk our hands into the mud, we straightened up – and while they were still all gawking at us we went splat, right in their faces.

'Have a big laugh then,' said Ruby – and we ran.

They started running after us, but we can be very speedy so we soon got clean away. Well. I wasn't clean. I was still covered in mud.

· 'But so are they!' Ruby spluttered breathlessly. 'Their faces. Oh, Garnet, that was so glorious. Twin-grin!'

'Twin-grin,' I echoed obediently, though I didn't really feel like smiling.

We have this little grinning ritual whenever we're really pleased about something. Ruby puts her fingers at the corners of my mouth and turns it into a huge grin, while I reach out at the same time and do the same to her.

I managed to stay grinning like a Halloween pumpkin, but I kept looking behind me all the same, in case those children might be creeping up on us.

'Relax. They'll have gone back to their stupid fishing,' said Ruby, sussing that I was still scared.

'Maybe. But they'll still be out to get us sometime, won't they,' I said stiffly, trying to keep my grin in place.

'Well, we'll get them back,' said Ruby airily. 'Especially that Big Blobby one.'

'But they'll all start hating us then. And we've got to go to school with them, haven't we,' I said. My grin wavered, and then drooped.

'We won't go to this dumb old school. We'll slope off by ourselves,' said Ruby.

'But they'll find out and we'll get into trouble,' I said. 'And we're in pretty big trouble now. We can't go home because Rose will get us, and we can't go down by the river because those children will get us.'

It looked like we were stuck for ever, hiding up a little alleyway at the edge of the village. I leant against the wall, the cold pebbly stuff scratching me through my T-shirt. My jeans were still wet and sticky with mud. My face ached with trying to smile. My eyes stung with trying not to cry again.

'Garnet?' said Ruby gently.

She put her arm round me and cuddled me close. I snuggled up against her and we held on tight to each other. Our shadows became Siamese.

'Perhaps we'd better go back to the bookshop,' I said eventually.

'No, not yet. We've only been gone an hour or so. She'll just get angry. No, we have to stay away ages and ages, and then she'll be really worried. Better to stay away until after Dad gets back, then he'll be dead worried too, and they'll maybe have a go at each other. Then when we do turn up they'll be so relieved we've not been kidnapped or killed that they won't go on at us. Or not so much, anyway.'

'But what are we going to do?' I wailed.

62

'We'll do one of our plays,' said Ruby.
That made me cheer up. Ruby hasn't felt
like playing one of our pretend games for ages.
So we had this really great game together.

And then, when we eventually sloped back
to the shop, Rose didn't get cross with us.
She'd done all the front of the shop by
herself, but she didn't tell on us to Dad. She
even washed out my jeans for me without
getting fussed. Gran would have gone nuts.

What's the matter with you, Garnet? Have
you gone completely nuts? Is this Let's Love
Rosy-Posy Day?

No. I can't stick her, you know that. But I'm
just trying to write a truthful account, that's
all. In our accounts book.

Well, I think we should give a good account of ourselves. And make a bad account of everyone else. That's much more fun.

Rose was OK when that woman in the quilty jacket and the lollopy dog came to complain about the red paint.

Dad looked like he was going to burst into tears, but Rose went 'Oh B-B-B-R-R-R-R-R-R-R-R-R!', blowing this giant raspberry and said it was our shop and we could paint it whatever colour we fancied and that the video shop two doors along with all its placards didn't exactly add to the authentic Victorian charm of the village anyway. So the bossy lady got into a huff and flounced out with her floppy dog and we were all laughing—

Yes, but Rose wasn't really that clever, because how many real customers has Dad had?

Well, there was the man who wanted the gardening book . . . and the lady who wanted all the Bills and Moons . . . lots of ladies . . .

Yes, but they only spend fifty pence at a time!

That vicar came. And he bought a Bible – the big one with pictures that cost heaps.

And that's about *it*. They don't want to come, the villagers. They don't like us. Or they don't like books. Or both.

Yes, but Dad says he's really after the Tourist Trade. The people who come at weekends. And holidaymakers.

Who'd ever want to come and have a holiday in this old dump? All right, the shop did get quite busy last Saturday and Sunday, but hardly anybody *bought* anything.

There were the hikers

and they left mud all over the place. There were the bikers

and they dripped ice-cream everywhere.
And there was that family who asked to
use the toilet.

None of that lot bought a sausage.

One of the bikers bought an old Beano
annual.

Oh, big deal. I'm telling you, Garnet. Dad's
going to go bust in six months.
Come on, let's play. Make the most of our
free time. Because we're starting at our new
school on Monday, yuck yuck yuck.

SIX

It's awful. We knew it would be. It's like a
little toy school. There's hardly any
playground. There aren't any computers.
There isn't even a television. The teacher
writes stuff up on a blackboard and we sit at
these dinky little desks with lids and
inkwells. It's like the sort of classroom you
get in a cartoon.

1 × 13 = 13
2 × 13 = 26
3 × 13 = 39
4 × 13 = 52

*Miss Debenham isn't a bit like that, Ruby!
This is Miss Debenham.*

Yes, and she made me feel positively sick
and squirmy inside when she stood us in
front of the class and introduced us – and as
if we *needed* introducing anyway. We're
famous in this dreary dump of a village.
Everyone knows us.

Especially Jeremy Treadgold and his gang.

Fancy that great Blob being in our class.
It's a wonder he can cram himself into the
teeny-weeny desk. Imagine having to sit next
to him.

*I'm glad we can sit together, anyway. Miss
Debenham asked us what we'd prefer.
Teachers don't usually ask you stuff like that,*

*they just tell you what they want you to do.
And I like some of the lessons, like when we
had to write about twins.*

You can be a real smarmy little creep at
times! I had it all sussed out.

THE GOOD THINGS ABOUT BEING A
TWIN

Everything

THE BAD THINGS ABOUT BEING A TWIN

Nothing

And then you were supposed to do your
mirror-writing trick. It would have been so
brilliant:

THE GOOD THINGS ABOUT BEING A
TWIN

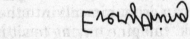

THE BAD THINGS ABOUT BEING A TWIN

Nothing

It would have been PERFECT. An answer, and a twin answer. Identical, like us.

But oh no, Miss Suck-up-to-the-teacher-smarty-farty has to write all that rubbish.

THE GOOD THINGS ABOUT BEING A TWIN

There are lots and lots of good things about being a twin. You're never alone, you've always got a best friend to talk to and play with. You can have all sorts of special secrets and make up wonderful games that no-one else can ever understand. You can say things together and do things together so that you can have twice the power.

THE BAD THINGS ABOUT BEING A TWIN

There aren't many bad things about being a twin. Just occasionally it might be peaceful to be alone. Not to have to talk or make up games or listen to secrets. Just to be yourself. Not part of anyone else. You.

Very *bad*, Garnet! Do you *really* want to be left alone? OK, I'll run off the next time that Big Blob tries to get us.

Oh, that was so awful! He crept up on us with this huge great wiggly worm in either hand, and I can't stand worms.

71

Well, I'm not absolutely enchanted with them myself. Especially not squirming down my jumper. But I got mine out. I shoved it straight down the Big Blob's trousers!

Judy said he once put a worm down her neck too. Judy just about went bananas. She said—

I'm not the slightest bit interested in Judy and what she said. I don't know why you wanted to go off with her.

She's quite nice, Ruby, really she is. And I didn't go off with her, you know that. Miss Debenham said she wanted us to do this big Noah's Ark painting to brighten up the classroom wall and she was going round the whole form asking them which animal they wanted to paint, and I kept hoping nobody else would bag a giraffe, because they're our favourite animal, so when she got to us I said, 'Giraffe' quick. And Miss Debenham smiled at you too and said, 'And you'll do a twin giraffe, right, Ruby?'

So I said, 'Wrong, Miss Debenham. I don't want to paint any stupid old giraffe.'

But why did you say that? And why did you have to choose a flea for your animal?

Simple. One little blob. Flea finished. And if you'd only shut up and waited for *me* to answer old Dumbo Debenham, you could have done a flea too. Then we could have just sat and mucked around for the rest of the lesson. But oh no, you have to go off with that ghastly Judy girl and paint stupid giraffes with her.

I didn't go off – well, not deliberately. I couldn't help it that Judy said she wanted to do a giraffe too. And I tried to back out, you know I did. But Miss Debenham said, 'No, come on, Garnet, you said you'd like to do a giraffe. So you can do the giraffes with Judy. Never mind what Ruby wants to do.'

Yes, never mind *me*.

Oh, Ruby. Don't be like that.

I'll be exactly how I want. If you want to pal around with Judy then fine, you go off with her.

I don't want to pal around with her.

So why did you let her tag around with us at playtime then? Going gab gab gab until I felt like punching her in the gob.

Well, what could I do? I couldn't tell her to go away.

I could.

You did. You were ever so rude to her. And I keep telling you, Ruby, she's good fun, she really is – you'd like her if you could bother to get to know her.

I'm not going to get to know any of them. OK. You go and have good fun with your super new friend. Pal around with her all you like. Just don't expect to pal around with *me*.

Ruby! Don't let's quarrel. I hate it so. Ruby, come back. Please.

SEVEN

Ruby?

I can't STAND it when Ruby won't talk to me. It's as if most of me goes missing. As if my own mouth won't work, my own hands won't hold.

She's right. I was crazy to write that stuff about being a twin. It's awful being on your own.

Ruby wouldn't talk to me all yesterday evening. When I tried saying anything she put

her hands over her ears and went Bla-bla-bla
so she couldn't hear.

After we'd had tea, Ruby went up to our
room and started reading an old Beano
annual. I said I was sorry, but she didn't look
up. I tried putting my arm round her but she
wriggled away. I took hold of the Beano
annual to make her look at me but she
grabbed it back and hit me on the head with
it. It hurt quite a lot, but that wasn't really
why I was crying.

Ruby didn't take any notice at all.

My nose started to run so badly that I had
to go and get a tissue. Rose saw me before I
could mop myself up.

'Oh, sweetie,' she said, and she pulled one of
her chiffony scarves off her neck and wiped
my nose with it. 'Hey, I'm just popping down
to that video shop because there's nothing
good on telly tonight. Come and help me
choose a good film, eh?'

I didn't know what to do. I knew Ruby would never forgive me if I palled up with Rose. But it didn't look like she would ever forgive me anyway.

'Come on, we'll get some chocs too,' said Rose. She rubbed her tummy. 'I've put on a good half-stone since we got here. Still, never mind, eh?'

I wanted to go with Rose. Ruby might not even know unless she looked out of our window. No, who was I kidding? It's like Ruby can look through a little window straight into my head.

'I'd better not,' I mumbled to Rose. 'I mean, I don't feel like it.'

'You don't always have to do what Ruby wants,' Rose said.

She can tell us apart now. Unless we deliberately trick her. She thinks she's getting to know us. But she can't ever really understand. I don't always get it myself. But I do have to do what Ruby wants. Because if I don't, this happens. And it's so horrid.

Rose usually chooses love films with big hunky men, but this time she brought back The Railway Children. *It's one of my all-time favourite films, but generally when we watch it Ruby mucks around and mocks all the accents and at the end when Bobbie runs to*

her father at the station and it's so lovely,
Ruby makes sick noises and switches it off
before it's finished.

Dad raised his eyebrows a bit when he saw
which film it was, but he didn't say anything.
He usually sits on the sofa with Rose, but this
evening he sat in the armchair and he caught
hold of me and sat me on his lap while Rose
put her feet up on the sofa, a box of Cadbury's
Dairy Milk balanced on her tummy. She kept
throwing Dad and me chocolates. I said I
wasn't very hungry thanks, but Dad popped
my favourite chocolate fudge into my mouth
as I spoke and I couldn't really spit it out.

They were being so nice to me, but it didn't
work. The chocolate didn't have any taste. The
Railway Children *got started but I couldn't*
watch it properly. I kept glancing up at the
ceiling, at Ruby crouched up above us all on
her own.

'Why don't we ask if she feels like coming
down now?' Rose said.

Dad and I looked at each other. Rose certainly doesn't understand Ruby yet.

Rose went up all the same. She left a couple of chocolates beside Ruby. They weren't touched when I came to bed.

Ruby and I always share the bathroom and do synchronized tooth-cleaning, but Ruby barged straight past me and banged the door in my face. When we got into our nighties in the bedroom she seemed to be staring straight through me, as if I didn't exist. That was exactly the way I felt.

When we were in bed with the light off I kept whispering to her, but she wouldn't answer. I lay awake for ages and ages and ages. In the middle of the night I slipped out of my bed and climbed in beside Ruby. She was snoring softly, deep in a dream, but she still wouldn't cuddle up

and after a while I crept back to my own bed.

*I think I slept a bit but now I'm wide awake
again, even though it's not properly morning.*

I think Ruby's awake too.

Ruby?

She's still not speaking.

But I know what to do now.

*I did it. And we're friends again now, aren't
we, Ruby?*

Yeah. OK, OK. Get *off* of me, Garnet!

*Make friends, make friends, never never
break friends?*

I said, didn't I?

*Write it too. Write it down here, in the
accounts book. Write that you'll never break
friends with me again.*

I will never break friends with my twin
sister and best friend Garnet Barker.

*Oh, you've really written it! And put: I
swear.*

I swear my twin sister and best friend
Garnet Barker is driving me completely batty
with all this sloppy junk, and if she doesn't
shut up soon I might well go back on my
promise.

You can't do that. No backsies.

I was only teasing, stupid. Here, what's all
this drivel you've been writing? Whimpering
on about me for page after page?

*Don't look at it now. You're right. It was just
rubbish.*

So you had chocolate fudge downstairs, did
you?

*I didn't mean to – I just had my mouth open
and—*

Oh, well. I might as well eat up my choccies too. One . . . Yum yum yum.

And two . . . Gobble, gobble, gobble. Don't look at me like that. You had yours last night.

Only one.

Well look, here . . .

It's all chewed and slobbery!

Well, we're twins, aren't we? Your slobber is the same as my slobber. My drool is the same as your drool. My spit is the same as your spit.

Your spit is a lot splashier than mine.

Hey, wasn't it great today when we got Jeremy Blob splat-splat! Oh boy oh boy! That was the most terrific supersonic idea of mine, eh? Going up to him in the playground and saying stuff ever so ever so softly so he shakes his head and screws up his face. 'What?' he says. 'I can't hear you?'

So we go, 'Then wash your ears out' and you spit . . . SPLAT. And *I* spit . . . SPLAT. In his ears.

I wish Miss Debenham hadn't been walking across the playground though. She wasn't very pleased either when I said I didn't want to

*finish my giraffe and I did a twin flea to
match yours. And Judy was a bit fed up too,
because now she's lumbered doing one and
three-quarters giraffes by herself.*

Still, we don't care, do we?

*It doesn't matter, so long as we've got each
other.*

So now school's a doddle, because Garnet
and I don't do anything. We just sit looking
blank when Dumbo Debenham gets on to us.
Or I write the barest minimum and Garnet
does mirror-writing. Or we copy everything
twice – two lots of sums, two maps, two fact-
sheets, because we say everything's got to be
doubled because we're a double ourselves.

'Double trouble,' said Dumbo Debenham,
and she sighed and tried separating us,
Garnet right at the back of the class and me
at the front.

It didn't work. Garnet just had to keep her
eye on me. I'd tilt my head one way, and that
was the signal to sneeze simultaneously. Or
I'd tilt my head the other way and we'd both
tip our books off the desk. Or I'd nod very
slightly and we'd both stand up and say in
unison, 'Please may I go to the toilet, Miss

Debenham?' and then we'd walk out keeping
step, me first, Garnet second, left right, left
right, our arms swinging right left, right left,
and then when I gave the slightest little
cough we'd toss our heads so that our plaits
would go left right, left right, over our
shoulders.

And all the kids would stare with their
mouths open.

We even spook Jeremy Blob!

But it looks like we're in double trouble
with Dad. Dumbo Debenham phoned him up
and told tales on us!

'So why are you acting so stupidly at
school?' Dad demanded.

'I think they act stupidly at home too!' said
Rose.

'We only act–'

'Stupid—'

'To stupid—'

'People,' we said.

But then Dad shook us. Hard. I thought he might even bang our heads together.

'Stop it! I won't have you talking to Rose like that. What's the matter with you? I just don't get it. You've always been such good girls. Well, you've had your moments, Ruby, but you've never ever behaved as badly as this before. And you've both always done so well at school. I've been so proud of you. But now it sounds as if you're going out of your way to be as naughty and disruptive as possible. And you're not even trying to make friends with the other children. Miss Debenham says you've got into silly fights with some of the boys – and you really upset one of the girls yesterday. Judy someone?'

That was great. She was carrying on with this boring boring Noah's Ark nonsense and she'd just got started doing the giraffe's long neck with brown paint, so I got Garnet and we did our wanting-to-wee double act and then as we went out we both bumped into Judy accidentally on purpose and her giraffe ended up with this amazing corkscrew neck. Shame.

I couldn't help sniggering just thinking about it, and Dad got madder than ever.

Garnet spoilt it a bit because she started snivelling, as always. Then Dad sighed and said, 'Why do you always have to copy Ruby, Garnet? You obviously tried hard at school at first. But now you're starting to be just as naughty as Ruby.' And then he shook me a bit and said, 'Why can't you ever copy Garnet, Ruby?'

But Garnet was OK.

'I don't copy Ruby,' she said.

'I don't copy Garnet,' I said.

And then I sniffed because I knew Garnet was just about to, and I rubbed my dry eyes and she rubbed her wet ones, and then Garnet knew I'd stare at Dad defiantly with my chin up so she did too.

It unnerved Dad, even though he's used to us. But Rose clapped her hands.

'They ought to go on stage,' she said.

'Well ha ha ha, we're going to,' I said.

Garnet was a bit slow with her response this time. She only managed a '. . . going to,' and she sounded a bit half-hearted. But I'm her other half. The oldest biggest bossiest half. We have to do what I say.

EIGHT

This is it! Our Big Chance!

We were sitting in the kitchen on Saturday, mucking about. Dad was down in the shop. Rose had caught the early bus to the town. We had the place to ourselves. Garnet mixed up some flour and water and started making dinky little dough twins.

She even plaited their hair and gave them little laces in their trainers.

I said I wanted mine to have Doc Martens – all the better for kicking, ha ha – and I tried to change their shoes, but they wouldn't go right. So I squashed my twin up and started all over again, but it just went all blobby. I turned it into Jeremy Blob instead, while Garnet made another me. Then I got some toothpicks and tortured Jeremy Blob until he stopped looking like a doughboy and turned into a porcupine.

I got fed up with dough then and folded up

a newspaper and cut it out carefully the way
Gran showed us once and then, when I
unfolded it, there was this whole row of paper
dolls. The newspaper just happened to be
Rose's *Guardian* and she hadn't even opened
it yet. Tough.

I got a felt tip and started scribbling in eyes
and mouths and buttons down the front of
each little paper girl. I'm not dead artistic like
Garnet. I can't be bothered to be so finicky.

'I'm turning them all into twins,' I said.

I did a smily mouth for me and a little-o
anxious mouth for Garnet, and then a smiley
mouth for me and a . . .

And then I stopped, because I saw the word
Twin on the paper doll. I read her skirt and
then I ferreted around for the left-over paper
to try to read the rest. I got the Sellotape and
started trying to stick the whole bang-shoot
back together again.

'Yes, Rose is going to want to read that when she gets back,' Garnet mumbled, putting the finishing touches to the little dough me.

'Blow Rose reading it. *We've* got to read it!' I said, and I was so shaking with excitement that I stuck myself together with the Sellotape. 'Garnet, come and take a look at this! Oh boy! No, oh *girl*. Oh *twin* girl!'

'Whatever are you burbling about?' said Garnet. 'Hey, don't jog. Look, you've made me muck up your plait now.'

'Leave it. *Look!*'

I shoved the crumpled, Sellotaped sheet of paper in front of her nose.

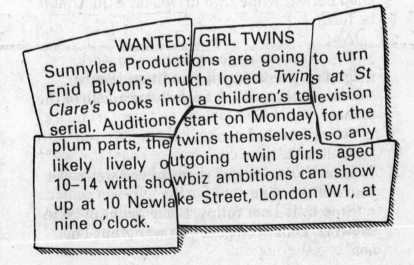

WANTED: GIRL TWINS
Sunnylea Productions are going to turn Enid Blyton's much loved *Twins at St Clare's* books into a children's television serial. Auditions start on Monday for the plum parts, the twins themselves, so any likely lively outgoing twin girls aged 10–14 with showbiz ambitions can show up at 10 Newlake Street, London W1, at nine o'clock.

'This is it, Garnet!' I shouted.

Garnet is usually a quick reader but she seemed to be taking her time getting through one small paragraph.

She was still holding the little dough me.

'Hey, watch out! You're spoiling me,' I said.

Garnet squashed me into a little ball and then dropped me on the kitchen floor.

'No,' she said.

'What?'

'No. I can't.'

'What do you *mean*? We can we can we can. Yes, all right, it's going to be difficult getting to London by nine o'clock. We'll have to get up ever so early. Rose will have to look after the shop herself while Dad drives us. Still, that'll be fun.'

'*No.*'

'Yes. Now, we're going to have to work mega-fast preparing our audition number. Get the book, quick, and we'll learn one of the scenes.'

'Ruby, I can't. I can't act for toffee, you know I can't.'

'Look, it'll be fine. I promise you won't wet yourself this time.'

'Stop it. It's not funny. I don't *want* to be in showbiz. Look, you go if you want, but I'm not.'

'Oh ha ha, very helpful. How can I audition as a twin by myself, eh? Take one of the little dough twins along with me? Don't be such a dope. Now, where's the book, we've got to get cracking. Which twin is which? I'll be the one that says the most. We'll work it so you don't have to say hardly anything, OK?'

'No, Ruby, please, *please*.' Garnet started scrabbling at me, getting dough all over my jumper.

'We can't miss out on this, Garnet. It's our big chance. We've got to go for it.'

'But it says lively. I'm not a bit lively. I don't jump about like you, I just sort of flop in a corner. And I'm not outgoing. I'm as inwardbeing as you could possibly get.'

'You'll be OK. Just copy me.'

Why do I always have to copy Ruby?
I can't act.
I don't want to act.
I can't go to an audition in London! I can't say a lot of stuff with everyone watching. It'll be even worse than being a sheep. Why won't Ruby understand? She won't listen to me. She's riffling through The Twins at St Clare's *right this minute, trying to choose which bit we'll act out.*
Only I'm not going to act.

I can't can't can't act.

Remember what Gran says? There's no such word as can't! Now stop scribbling and start spouting. We've got to be word-perfect by Monday!

It's OK! I don't have to act after all. Dad won't let us.

I can't believe he could be so Mega-Mean. He doesn't seem to see this is our one big chance, tailor-made for us. He won't even take it seriously.

'Don't be daft, Ruby. As if I'm going to drive you all the way to London at the crack of dawn on Monday! And I don't want you and Garnet involved in any acting caper while you're still children. I can't stick those simpering stage-school kiddiewinks. You're already enough of a show-off as it is.'

What a CHEEK! He can't be bothered to help us achieve our all-time ambition

Your *ambition*

and yet look what we've had to do for him. We've had to leave Gran and all our friends and our old school and come and live in this horrible dusty old dump in the middle of the boring bleak rainy old country which is all mud and sheep and nothing else and he says we've got to have old Rosy Ratbag as our *mother*.

Stepmother. And Rose said she didn't fancy herself as a stepmother anyway, and she didn't want us to feel she was forever trying to slip us poisoned apples. She said she just wanted to be our friend.

Well, we don't ever ever ever want to be friends with her. Do we? *Do we, Garnet?*

I suppose not. No. But she's not really as bad as all that. And she said she didn't see why we couldn't go to the audition. She said she thought we'd walk away with the parts.

She told Dad not to be so stuffy. She said she'd even get up early on Monday and drive us in the van.

Yes, but she didn't really mean it. She knew Dad would put his foot down and say no.

Still, she did stick up for us.

Look, what is this, the Rosy Ratbag Appreciation Society? You'll be writing a fanzine about her next.
Save your appreciation for *us*.

The talented gems of stage and screen, identical twins Ruby and Garnet Barker, who first sprang to stardom in the acclaimed television serial, 'The Twins at St Clare's'.

Only we're not going to be in The Twins at St Clare's.

Oh yes we are.

Dad won't let us. He won't ever change his mind. He's like you. He won't take us.

I know he won't take us. So we'll take ourself.

What???

I'll fix it. We *can't* miss this chance. Come on, Garnet. Twin-grin. *Smile.*

Ruby won't be able to fix it – will she???

I DID FIX IT!!!
I prodded my brainbox into action and charged out on Saturday afternoon to arrange things. I phoned the station to check on train times.
I went into the video shop and ordered the taxi for quarter past five on Monday morning. Mr Baines the video man is also the taxi man. *And* he's also a nosy old git who wanted to know why we were going to the station to catch the early train. I spun him this tale

about it being Gran's birthday. He seemed to take it for granted that Dad was going to be visiting her too.

Then I went to the nearest antique shop and tried to sell my silver locket and my wristwatch and a dopey old china baby doll that Gran gave me. I never liked it even when I was little. Garnet played with mine as well as hers. But the doll *was* mine. And the locket and the watch. But the antique shop lady wouldn't buy them. She said I had to have Mummy or Daddy with me.

Well, I haven't *got* a mummy. Or much of a dad.

I tried the next antique shop. No go. And the last one. Useless.

But did I give up? Nope. I went to the car-boot sale in the field by the river on Sunday morning. No-one was very interested in my chain and my watch but I saw them get excited about the doll, even though they tried to act like they couldn't be bothered. They offered me a fiver like they were doing me a favour. I'm not daft. I asked for fifty. Of course they didn't *give* me fifty. But they gave me twenty.

Which wasn't going to be enough for the taxi and the train fare, even with all our savings in our piggybank, so when my alarm

went off at four in the morning I sneaked
downstairs while Garnet was still asleep and
pinched a note or two out the till. It isn't
really stealing if it's your own family, is it? If
you're going to pay them back anyway? Well,
all right, it is – but I *had* to.

Then I went and woke Garnet and we
bumbled about in the dark getting ready, in
our best clothes

and then we crept downstairs and snaffled
some biscuits for breakfast and then stood
outside the front door waiting for Mr Baines
so that he wouldn't ring the bell and wake
Dad or Rosy Ratbag. They were still fast
asleep. I checked.

Mr Baines was ten minutes late so I was in a bit of a tizzy in case we were going to miss the train, and then he held things up by asking where Dad was, and he's got this incredibly loud voice and I was sure he was going to wake everyone up. But I rose to the occasion. I spun him this story about Dad having a tummy bug and being unable to travel, but Gran was so disappointed when he rang her that he promised to send us on our own.

'Two little girls like you?' said Mr Baines doubtfully, but I showed him my bulging purse and told him Gran was meeting us off the train, so he shrugged and said OK.

Garnet didn't say a word. She still seemed half-asleep. Then she went green in the taxi. *I'm* the one who gets travel-sick, but I was perfectly OK. I even remembered to give Mr Baines a tip, thought I didn't think he really deserved it, being late and asking hundreds of questions all the way.

I bought the tickets for the train. Garnet wasn't with me. She was being sick behind a hedge. I was worried she might muck up her best jacket. You can't audition attractively with vomit all down your front. But she was quite neat about it, though she looked greener than ever when she came back. Still, our jackets are green, so at least she matched.

She was all shivery, even on the train. I made her rehearse a bit and she got even more trembly and tearful.

'Don't you dare cry,' I said. 'You don't want to be all red-eyed and bleary at the audition.'

She did cry a bit even so, but I mopped her up in the ladies loo.

'You're not going to let me down, are you, Garnet?' I said very fiercely.

Sometimes you've got to be fierce to get what you want. But even I felt a bit timid when we got off the train because it was all so big and busy and we didn't know where to go and we asked someone where Newlake Street was and they'd never even heard of it, and I said we'd get a tube but we didn't know which tube, or where, and we went down the escalator and then back up the escalator and then I saw a taxi sign and we still had some money in our purse so we took a taxi.

It turned out we didn't have quite enough money after all. The taxi driver got a bit narked.

But I wasn't bothered about that. I was bothered about something else. I got out of the taxi and Garnet staggered out after me. And we stared. And hundreds of eyes stared back at us. Twin eyes. Twin after twin after twin after twin.

NINE

It was so weird seeing so many twins. Ruby
and I have seen identical twins before,
obviously, but never hundreds of pairs. It was
as if the whole world had split into two. I felt
as if I was splitting too. We've always felt so
different. Unique. Special. It's what made us
us. But standing there in that street we were
just part of the crowd. Totally ordinary. With
nothing at all to make us stand out.

'Let's go back home,' I said to Ruby. 'Look at
them all. We don't stand a chance.'

'Don't be so ridiculous,' said Ruby furiously.
'I keep telling and telling and telling you, this
is our big chance. We're not giving up now.
We'll show them all. We'll act better than any
of them.'

'But I can't act at all, Ruby.'

She just gave me this terrible look, took
hold of my arm, and marched me to the end of
the very long queue.

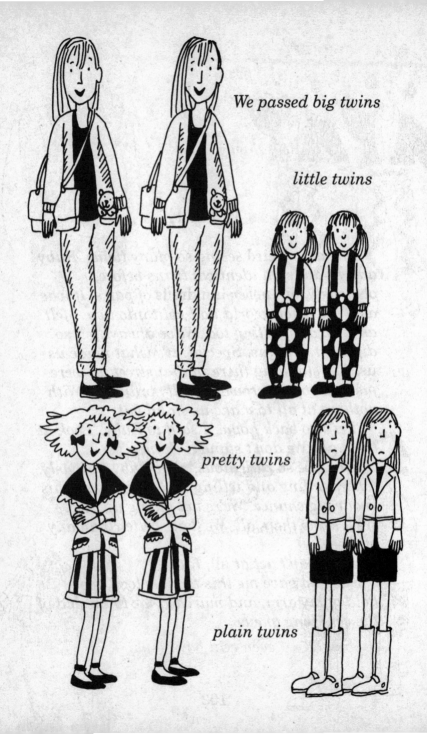

We passed big twins

little twins

pretty twins

plain twins

showy twins

shabby twins

girly-girly twins

tomboy twins

even real boy twins.

'They obviously haven't even read the book!' said Ruby dismissively. 'Unless they're going to put on frocks and wigs and play the parts in drag.'

'But look at some of the others. The ones with the big smiles and loud voices. I bet they've been to acting school,' I said.

'Well, so what. I've done my best to school you in acting. Now come on, let's go over our parts.'

'Not out here, in front of everyone,' I said, agonized.

'Look, you're the one who needs heaps of practice, not me,' said Ruby. Then she pulled me close and muttered in my ear, 'We'll just do it in whispers, OK? And I've been thinking – we'll have to inject a little ooomph into our act to make us stand out in front of all these others. So we'll still do the scene with the twins having a battle with Mam'zelle, but we'll act Mam'zelle too. Don't look so scared, I'll do her. I am good at doing zee French accent, ma cherie, oh la la, très bon.'

But it turned out we didn't get a chance to do any of our act. We had to wait hours and hours in the queue and I was desperate to go to the loo so when we did eventually get inside the building I had to walk around with my legs crossed and we had to give our names

and addresses and date of birth and school to
this lady at a desk and then we went upstairs
and I was scared I might really wet myself
and it would be the sheep situation all over
again only worse but there were toilets along
the corridor

and a big cloakroom where you were supposed
to change only we didn't have anything to
change into, 'cos we were wearing it. But Ruby
pinched my cheeks to give me a bit more
colour and I tidied our hair although my
hands were trembling so I could barely tie a
knot and then we got into another queue,

waiting to get into the actual audition room.

It got scarier and scarier and I had to dash
back to the loo once or twice and even Ruby
got a bit fidgety and she kept staring round at
all the other twins. They were rehearsing their
routines and they all seemed so brilliant

that Ruby started to frown and bite her nails.

'I didn't figure we might have to dance,' she
mumbled. 'They don't do any dancing in the
story do they? Although maybe they're turning
it into a musical version? So if we're asked,
we'll sing . . . er . . . not a pop song, they'll all
do that. We could do "My Bonnie Lies Over the
Ocean" with hand gestures.'

'I'm not singing, especially not with gestures!' I said. 'You know we can't sing in tune, either of us.'

'Well, we could just sort of say the words, with lots of expression,' said Ruby relentlessly. 'And if we have to dance well . . . we'll just have to jump and jiggle a bit. Improvise. You copy me, OK?'

This was so obviously not OK that I didn't even bother to protest.

'We could work on a routine now, you know,' said Ruby, hopping and skipping and kicking out one leg.

She kicked a little too enthusiastically, and there was an argument with the twins in front of us.

They were dressed up in wonderfully old-fashioned school uniform – gymslips and baggy blouses and lisle stockings and strappy

shoes. One of the lisle stockings had a little
ladder now where it had connected with
Ruby's kick, and the mother of the laddered-
lisle was very cross indeed.

'Look, it was an accident – anyway, it just
adds to her general schoolgirl . . .authenticity,'
said Ruby, pronouncing this big word with
pride.

The mother didn't seem convinced, and the
schoolgirl twins were still getting all shirty
too, but then they were called into the audition
room so they rushed off in a fluster.

'Us next,' said Ruby. She took hold of me by
the shoulders. 'We're going to do great, Garnet.
Better than any of this dopey stupid showy-
offy lot. You and me. Ruby and Garnet. We'll
act it all out and it won't be scary at all, it'll
just be like us playing in private at home.
Trust me.'

I tried. And then it was our turn. And it
wasn't at all like playing in private. We were
shown on to this stage and there were lots of
people watching us and a camera filming us
and I was so frightened I nearly fell over.
Ruby grabbed me by the hand and hissed
'Twin-grin' and marched us into the middle of
the stage.

'Hi, twins,' said this woman with short hair
and a smock.

'Hi there,' said Ruby, imitating her voice,
trying to sound all cool and casual, though I
could see little beads of sweat on her forehead.
She nudged me, and I squeaked 'Hi' too.
'We've got our audition piece all prepared,'
Ruby said brightly, trying to show them we
were dead professional. 'I'm Pat and she's
Isabel and I'm also Mam'zelle and at the end
I'm Janet as well.'

They all laughed, for some reason. I
blushed, because I was scared they thought
Ruby was silly, but Ruby didn't seem to mind.
She laughed too.

'We'd love to see your little number some time, twins, but right now we just want to test out your voices,' said the woman with the short hair. 'Sooo – twin number one. Tell me what you had to eat yesterday.'

Ruby blinked at her. But then she threw back her hair, put her hand on one hip, and got started.

'OK, you want to know what I had to eat yesterday. Well, breakfast was boring old muesli again. Garnet and I used to have Coco Pops and jam sandwiches and they were yummy, but now we have this awful woman living with us, our dad's girlfriend, and she's into health foods so it's bye-bye Coco Pops, hello muesli – all this oat and bran that makes your face ache munching and then there are these little raisins like rabbit droppings, yuck.'

They were all laughing again, but this time even I could see that this was good. They loved Ruby.

'Right, now, twin two, tell us what you had for lunch,' said the woman with short hair.

They stopped looking at Ruby. They looked at me. And Ruby looked at me too. Desperately. Terrified I was going to let us down.

I tried to pretend to myself that I wasn't shy

stupid scaredy-cat Garnet. I made out I was Ruby. I threw back my hair. I put my hand on my hip. I opened my mouth to start.

I had it all worked out what I was going to do. I was going to tell about Rose's garlic crumble and how it not only tasted absolutely disgusting, but people ducked and dodged for days afterwards whenever we breathed in their direction and we'd worn out six toothbrushes already trying to take the taste away. I could be funny too if I really tried. I could be just as good as Ruby. I could.

But then someone came bursting through the door and stood there, staring. Dad!

And I couldn't. I simply couldn't.

He didn't say anything to stop me.

But he didn't need to. I couldn't get started, not in front of him. I opened my mouth – but nothing came out. I tried to speak, but I couldn't even squeak.

'Come on, *Garnet,' said Ruby.*

I gulped, I opened my mouth, I tried. But all I managed was a goldfish impersonation.

'Look, I'll say what we had for lunch,' said Ruby.

'No, sweetie, we've already heard you. We want your twin to talk now. Let's skip lunch. And tea and supper. What time did you go to bed, twin two?'

I saw Ruby flash her eyes at me. I knew she was willing me to tell a funny story about our bed-delaying tactics, our constant unnecessary trips to the bathroom, our midnight raids on the fridge, our frequent nocturnal ramblings – all deliberately done to unnerve Dad and Rose, so that they could never totally relax into unwedded bliss.

I could tell it, but not in front of Dad.

So, after several centuries had gone by and I actually saw the short-haired woman glance at her watch, I started a stupid mumble about 'Well, we're supposed to start getting ready for bed at nine, ten at weekends, but we often try to stay up.'

My voice was this sad expressionless little squeak. I saw Ruby close her eyes in agony. I saw Dad hang his head. I saw the short-haired woman and all her colleagues shaking their heads. I saw it all and I shrank down to mouse-size to match my squeak.

'Thank you, sweetie. Off you go, twins. Next!' said the short-haired woman. She was already staring past us, smiling at the new set of twins.

'No, hang on a minute!' said Ruby. 'Look my sister isn't very well, she's been sick, she's not normally like this, she can speak up and be ever so funny, I swear she can. How about if we just do a couple of minutes of our prepared piece? Give us a chance. We've used up all our savings getting here, and we're going to get in terrible trouble with our dad when we get back . . .'

'Yes, it's a shame, sweetie, but we don't really have the time,' said the short-haired woman, and she put her arm round both of us. It wasn't just sympathy. She propelled us gently but firmly to the edge of the stage.

Even in the midst of her despair Ruby remembered the camera, twisting round and grimacing in agony, and then she sighed and waved her hand.

I could hear a few chuckles.

'That kid's a caution,' said someone.

'Yeah. Pity about her twin.'

It was only a murmur. But it was like a giant roaring in my ears. It wouldn't soften or stop.

*I couldn't seem to hear properly even when
Dad caught up with us.*

*'You bet you're in terrible trouble,' he said
furiously. 'How* dare *you run off here like this,
when I expressly forbade it. I couldn't believe
it when we woke up and found you both gone.
I was so worried I was going to call the police,
but Rose insisted you'd both be all right and
that you'd obviously gone for this idiotic
audition.'*

*'Well, it was a complete waste of time
anyway,' said Ruby. 'You really blew it for us,
Dad. We were doing just great and then you
had to come barging in and put us off our
stroke.'*

'Put me *off. Not you,' I said. 'And it wasn't
Dad's fault. He waited. He gave us a chance.
But I mucked it up. That's what they said. You
were great, Ruby, yeah. But I was useless.
They said so.'*

*'No they didn't,' said Ruby. 'And anyway,
they didn't give you a proper chance. It wasn't
fair.'*

*'You don't want to be an actress anyway,
Garnet,' said Dad. 'And even if you'd both
been offered the parts, I wouldn't have let you
take them. Ruby can act when she grows
up, but I don't want my girls turning into*

ghastly little child stars, thank you very much.'

'There's no chance of me being any sort of star,' I said, and I started crying. I couldn't bear it. They were both so sorry for me. Dad was still mega-mad because we'd sneaked off up to London by ourselves, but he was holding back his anger for a bit to try to comfort me.

And Ruby wasn't cross with me. She should hate me for ever because I did muck it up. I should have said all that stuff and never mind about Dad being there. I could have done. Only I didn't. I let her down. I'll always let her down.

She's the biggest and the brightest and the best.

She's the caution.

She's the star.

It's a pity she's stuck with me.

Pity about her twin.

Pity about her twin.

Pity about her twin.

TEN

What's all this pity piffle??? Perlease, Garnet!
And anyway, I did get cross with you. I had a
real go at you in the car, because you *were* a
bit of a wally at the audition. What did it
matter if Dad was there or not? You could
have made something up if you didn't want to
do a rant at Rose. I mean, I wouldn't go on at
you if I truly thought you couldn't do it, but
you *can*. Well, you could have. Only it's too
late now. We've blown it. Lost our chance. We
don't get to be famous child stars. We're drab
child nobodies stuck in this dreary dump for
ever and ever. *And* we've lost all our savings
for nothing. Not to mention my baby doll that
Gran gave me.

Garnet? Oh, don't start crying *again*.

Look, *I'm* the one who should be crying.
I'm the one who wants to act. *I'm* the one that
Dad is maddest at. The way he went on and
on at me! And then when I argued back and

told him he was an old worryguts and that we're big enough to look after ourselves and what possible harm could happen on a simple trip to London, I thought he was actually going to clock me one.

He hasn't ever smacked us, has he? I wish he would, then we could show the bruises at school and get taken into care.

I mean it. I'm sick of living here with him and her.

Hey, let's write to Gran and see if she could possibly squeeze us into her flat. We could sleep curled up on her settee, couldn't we? And she keeps saying how much she misses us on her postcards.

Then we could go back to our old school. We're not going to this stupid new school again, especially now that Dumbo Debenham's told tales on us. We're not going even if Dad picks us up and tries to drag us there. We're not speaking to him, right? And we're certainly not speaking to *Rose*. Who cares if she came out with all that guff about us being ultra-determined and clever getting ourselves to London. We didn't ask her to stick up for us, did we?

Garnet? Look, what does it matter what she's shouting? We don't want to go and watch television with her! Who cares if it's—

It was us! Well, only a glimpse, but they showed me, doing my goodbye bit. The camera came right up close. They didn't show much of Garnet, just a bit of her hair and an elbow but they showed all of me, and there was a voice-over saying, 'And this twin certainly took rejection like a trouper.'

Pity they didn't say our names. Still. We were on the telly. Well, I was.

It was on the News. We missed the first part but Rose videoed it. They did a whole little item about the audition for the *Twins at St Clare's* series as a clever early puff for the programme, seeing as it's going to be made by the same telly company. They showed some of those other twins doing their party pieces. There weren't any as good as us. Well, me. Of course, that's only my opinion.

The twins that they've chosen are absolutely *awful*.

That's the way they talk,too. Oooh absolutely jolly good show, fwightfully, ya, jolly super-duper green-welly wallies.

Perhaps it's just as well we weren't chosen. If they'd got us to talk all twiddly-snooty-pop like that then we'd have been sent up rotten for ever and a day. Kids won't want to watch a pathetic programme like that. Or if they do, they'll just laugh at it.

Still, it looks like they're pulling out all the stops on the production. It's being filmed on location in this real big boarding school during the summer holidays. They showed all the grounds. It was just like a stately home. And there was a swimming pool. And a sort of

miniature zoo, where they keep their pets.
And inside this huge great house it wasn't a
bit like a *school* school. There were ordinary
boring old classrooms but they had playrooms
with television and videos and music centres
and computers and upstairs there weren't
dormitories like I thought – they had lots of
bedrooms with flowery duvets and teddies on
the beds and posters up on the walls, and
best of all, this school has its own *theatre*. It's
quite small, OK, but it's got a real stage with
red velvet curtains and lighting and props
and everything, and they put on plays.

I wish we could go to a school like that.

Hey.

Wow.

Yes!

No!

Oh, Garnet, come on! It would be absolutely
fantastic! Oh, let's go there. We wouldn't be
acting, we'd be the *real* twins of St Clare's.
Well, Marnock Heights. It would be such fun.
We could play all those posh games – hockey
and lacrosse and cricket in the summer. I bet
I'd be absolutely ace at cricket. And we could
have a pet each in the little zoo place. Twin
pets.

Rabbits? Those little ones with shy faces. Dwarf rabbits.

OK, twin baby bunnies. Though I'd sooner have gerbils. Or rats.

I don't like rats. Or gerbils. I don't even like mice.

Right, we're agreed. It's rabbits. We'll go and play with our rabbits every day and we'll have a game of cricket and we'll swim in the pool and in the evenings we'll watch videos in

the sitting-room and then, after we've gone to
bed, we'll have mega-midnight feasts.

This is a game, isn't it?

No! It can be real. We're going to go to
boarding school.

*Yes, it's a school, so there'll be lessons all
day. We can't just muck about stroking our
rabbits and playing games. There'll be
English and History and Technology. And
hard stuff too like Geometry and Latin.*

That's OK. You'll be able to do that. And did

you see that library in the telly clip? All those wonderful books, Garnet.

We've got books here.

Old boring books. We hate this bookshop. We hate this school and this whole horrible dump of a village. So we're going to get out. We're going to go to boarding school. Marnock Heights. We'll write a letter applying. You'd better do it, Garnet, your writing's much neater than mine. I'll tell you what to put.

But I don't want to—

I'm sick of you going on about what you want and don't want. Look, *I* wanted to be one of the twins of St Clare's on the television. *I* planned and plotted so that we got all the way to London by ourselves. *I* sold all my stuff. *I* did my audition thingy so well that they all laughed and they really liked me, and it looked like we'd actually got the part, didn't it? But then *you* mucked it up.

Yes.

There's no need to look like that. I'm not being deliberately horrid. I'm just trying to

get you to understand that it would be ultra
ultra ultra mean of you to muck up my
chances of getting what I want second best in
the world. Right?

The Red Bookshop
High Street
Cussop
19 May

Dear Madam - We are sorry, we don't know your name.

    We are ten-year-old identical twins,
nearly eleven and we hate our school in this
village. We don't fit in. The lessons are boring and
there aren't any proper books and the only games
we play are rounders.

    We went to the television audition for <u>The
Twins at St Clare's</u>. We very nearly got the part
actually. We were featured in the television coverage.
Well, one of us was. And you were featured too and
your wonderful school and we thought Oooh this is
our idea of heaven, the stage and the swimming pool
and the games and the animals and all that.

    So please can we come to your school in September?
We promise to be good pupils and you don't have to
worry about us being homesick because we hate
our home.   Yours faithfully
                 Ruby Barker
                 Garnet Barker.

P.S. Please say yes. You won't regret it. Honestly.

Look at this!

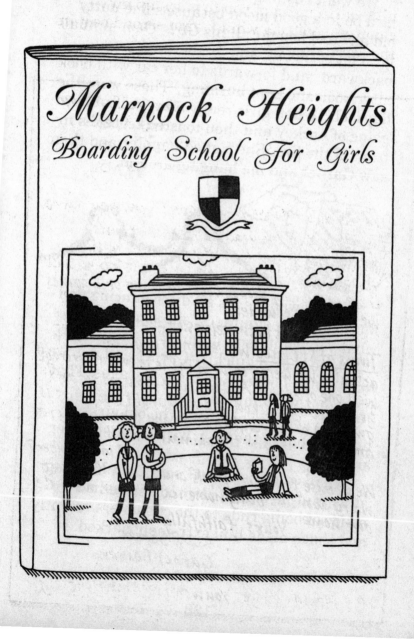

Marnock Heights
Boarding School For Girls

We went rushing to tell Dad. We thought he'd be in a good mood because some nutty old girl had bought all his *Girls' Own* annuals for a lot of money, and as she staggered backwards and forwards to her car with book after book she kept burbling, 'Those were the days, eh? When girls really *were* girls. A hard game of hockey and then toasted teacakes in front of the fire.' She sighed happily, and then saw Garnet and me hanging around.

'Only nowadays it's all disco dancing and McDonald's beefburgers,' she said. 'That's what you want, isn't it, girls?'

'Oh no,' I said quickly. 'Garnet and me, we'd like to play hockey and toast teacakes. That's just what we want too.'

'Well, good for you,' said the old girl, lurching out of the shop with the last of her annuals.

'What's all this about?' said Dad, blinking at us. But he looked pleased. We've had a policy of being rude to the customers recently and that's made him extremely narked. I looked at Garnet. She looked at me. I took a deep breath.

'We're not kidding, Dad. We read all the *St Clare's* books, see, when we were wanting to act in the telly series. And we think it all sounds really great. So Garnet and I want to go to boarding school.'

Dad laughed, not taking us seriously.

'It's not really like it is in books,' said Dad. 'I don't think either of you would go a bundle on real boarding school. You have to work hard and do as you're told all the time. According to poor Miss Debenham, you don't do any work at all and never ever do as you're told.'

'Yes, but that's because she's a silly teacher and it's a silly school. But if we went to a super top-notch boarding school then we'd be mega-good, really truly. A boarding school like Marnock Heights.'

'Like *where*?'

'It's the place they're using for the *St Clare's* film. It's a real school. And so Garnet and I wrote to the headmistress asking to go there and she's sent us this booklet all about it, look.'

I ran to fetch it and shoved it under Dad's nose.

'Oh, for goodness sake! Will you girls *stop*

doing things behind my back,' Dad groaned.

'Say we can go, though, Dad, *please*. You look at all the pictures. It's lovely, isn't it?'

'Oh, very lovely,' said Dad, flicking through. Then he stopped at the back page, where there were two pieces of paper tucked into a little pocket. 'And very lovely school fees too! Eight thousand a year. Each! Oh yes, nice one, Ruby.'

I stared at him and then snatched the paper. There were all these figures on it. The fees. I didn't realize you had to *pay* to go to some schools. You had to pay an enormous enormous enormous fee to go to Marnock Heights.

'Oh no,' I wailed.

'Oh no,' Garnet wailed too. But she didn't sound too fussed, in actual fact. Right, Garnet????

Well . . .

We've got to think POSITIVE. Because all is not lost. Maybe Dad won't have to fork out any fees. Not that he could anyway. We're far too poor. But But But . . . There was a letter tucked into the pocket of the prospectus, along with the note about the frightful fees.

Marnock Heights
Gorselea
Sussex

22 May

Dear Ruby and Garnet

What lovely names! You wrote me a
lovely letter too. I'm pleased that you'd
like to attend Marnock Heights. Here is
the current prospectus. Show it to your
parents or guardians.

I'd like to point out that we do
award several special scholarships each
year. These have already been awarded for
the new intake in the Autumn, but one
girl is now unable to take up her
scholarship because she's going abroad.
Perhaps you would like to come to the
school and sit the entrance examination
to see if either of you might pass highly
enough for scholarship consideration?

Please telephone my secretary for
an appointment.

With best wishes

Yours sincerely

Miss Jeffreys

Headteacher
(There, you know my name now!)

ELEVEN

Dad still wouldn't hear of it. At first. But we kept on at him.

You *kept on at him.*

On and on and on. And then he started to weaken.

It was Rose too. She said we should go for it. She said she wished she'd had a proper education.
'It's a great chance. It's ever such a famous school. If one of them got a scholarship there then they'd be able to go on, do anything, achieve anything.'

She's just desperate to get rid of us.
Because we're driving her crackers.

*You sometimes drive me crackers, Ruby. You
won't ever change your mind about anyone.*

Or anything. So we're going to Marnock
Heights!

*We're sitting the exam, that's all. And I
don't see the point, as there's two of us and
only one scholarship.*

We'll wangle two, somehow. Once Miss
Jeffreys gets to know us. She likes us already.
She's ever so complimentary in her letter.
We're lovely. I'm Miss Lovely Ruby and you're
Miss Lovely Garnet, OK? Oh, come *on*,
Garnet, cheer up! We've won! We've got our
own way!

*You've got your own way. And I'm worried
about the exam. She doesn't say what sort. If
it's an interview then I'm scared I'll go all
stupid and shy and not know what to say.
Like at the audition.*

It's OK, I'll do all the talking. You just
leave it to me.

So I left the talking to Ruby. We were shown into Miss Jeffreys' study and she shook our hands and smiled and gave us tea and biscuits and as we sipped and nibbled, Miss Jeffreys asked us questions.

They were really hard questions too, like:

'Why do you think education for girls is important?'

and 'What are your ambitions for the future?'

and 'What do you like doing in your spare time?'

and even 'How do you feel about being a twin?'

I feel bad about being a twin because I let Ruby down. I couldn't think of a thing to say. I just tagged on to the end of her sentences. She was brilliant.

Hmm! *Mega*-brilliant.

It was easy-peasy. I didn't say what I *really* think, naturally. I just said all this stuff to impress Miss Jeffreys and make her see that we are ideal pupils for Marnock Heights. I don't care a bit about education but I spouted stuff that old Rosy-Ratbag said the other day. And I said truthfully enough that our ambition is to be famous actresses, but I said we needed to study Shakespeare and if we stay in Cussop you don't even get *started* on Shakespeare until you go to sixth-form college. And I said that in our spare time we acted, and we also read lots, and I named all the books that Garnet likes, and some of Dad's Dickens and Hardy, and Miss Jeffreys looked dead impressed. She asked about the stories but I made some stuff up and I'm sure she swallowed it. And then when she asked about the twin bit I said it was just like being one person, only we were twice as good as anyone else.

She laughed and said that was a really good answer.

So *I* said that it was ever so important that we mustn't ever be separated and that as we always shared everything maybe we could share a scholarship too.

Dad got all fidgety then but she laughed even more. Then she took us all round the

school and the grounds, and it is truly
fantastic.

The other girls seem OK too. One looked a
bit snobby so I stuck my tongue out at her,
but she stuck her tongue out back at me and
then we both grinned. She had red hair and
little wicked eyes. I think we'll be friends
with her when we come to Marnock Heights.

If.

Look, I keep *telling* you, Garnet, we'll get
there. OK, we had to sit in the library and do
that boring old written exam – and I must
admit that got me a bit worked up because

that other teacher insisted that we sit at opposite ends so we couldn't work together the way we always do. That was ever so unfair. And then, when I caught your eye and we were sort of conferring, it was mean of that teacher to make me turn round and face the other way. They don't understand. We weren't cheating or anything. It's just the way we work, isn't it? Especially when it comes to all that boring stuff like arithmetic and general knowledge. And that composition was ultra-blobby-boring. 'Snow in Winter'! What did you write, eh?

You'll get mad at me.

Oh no. What did you put???

I just imagined a mountain all over with snow and what it must look like. And how odd it must be for the sheep, all green grass one minute and then white sharp stuff that hurts their teeth. And people always say there's a blanket of snow on the ground and yet if you were under that blanket, buried, you'd be dead. And how once when we were making snow angels in the park I stopped moving my arms and legs to see what it would feel like to be frozen. And snow looks so clean and pure but nothing's dirtier when everyone's trudged through it and it's all grey with yellow patches and how it's always like that, it can't ever stay the same, and yet each time you hope there'll be a way of keeping it looking beautiful.

Oh yucky yucky yuck! What did you have to write that rubbish for? I just bunged a few bits down about robins and icicles and footsteps crunching, like the verses inside Christmas cards. That's what they wanted, you idiot, not all your weirdo ramble.

I'm sorry, Ruby.

Yes, well, so you should be.

Ruby . . . What if you get accepted for the scholarship and I don't?

We're *both* going to get a scholarship.

But what if we don't? Would you go to Marnock Heights without me?

I keep telling and telling you, we're going together.

Yes, and I keep asking and asking . . . if it's

just you that gets accepted, will you go?

No. Yes. I don't *know.*

I think you should. Though it will be horrible without you. But I can't stand it if I'm always going to be the one that holds you back.

Marnock Heights

Gorselea
Sussex
29 May

Dear Mr Barker

I thoroughly enjoyed meeting you
and your delightful daughters last
week.
Ruby is a charming child, so
full of vim and vigour. No wonder
she wants to be an actress. I am
sure she will succeed in her
ambitions one day. I'm afraid we
can't offer her a scholarship at
Marnock Heights. She is obviously
witty and intelligent and her
conversation sparkles - though she
tends to get rather carried away and
bluffs when she's uncertain! Her
written work is lively if a little
slapdash, but I'm afraid she failed
several of our tests. If she could
only apply herself more vigorously
then I'm sure she could reach a far

We're not going to be held back, either of us. We're going rushing forwards. To Marnock Heights.

higher standard. I feel she's relied on her sister to do all her work for so long that she's failed to reach her full academic potential.

Garnet too might benefit from a term of separation from her sister. She lets Ruby do all her talking for her, and therefore does not interview at all well. However, she came into her own in the written tests. She has a few gaps in her knowledge but on the whole she did very well. Her essay was outstanding - extremely sensitive and mature. We would like to offer her a full scholarship at Marnock Heights, commencing in the Autumn term.

With best wishes

Yours sincerely

Miss Jeffreys

Headteacher

TWELVE

We couldn't believe it. We thought Miss Jeffreys had got us mixed up.

'She means me,' said Ruby. 'She must mean me.'

'Yes, it can't be me,' I said. 'Ruby will have got the scholarship.'

'No,' said Dad. 'It's definitely Garnet.'

'Let me see the letter!' Ruby demanded.

Dad didn't want either of us to see it.

'It's addressed to me,' he said. 'And it's plain what it says. There's no mix up.'

'She's just got our names round the wrong way,' Ruby insisted. 'It's always happening.'

'Not this time,' said Rose.

'Look, it's absolutely not fair if she's read the letter too, when it's got nothing to do with her. She's not our mother,' said Ruby.

'No, but I'm your father, and I want you to calm down, Ruby, and we'll talk all this over carefully.'

'Not till you show me the letter!'

'I'd show both the girls the letter,' said Rose. 'They're not little kids. I think they should see what it says.'

So Dad showed us.

It was like a smack in the face.

Not for me. For Ruby.

I read quicker than she does. I watched her face while she was finishing the letter. I couldn't bear it.

'She's written a whole load of rubbish,' I said quickly. 'She only met us for one afternoon and yet she thinks she knows us. Well she doesn't, does she, Ruby?'

Ruby was getting very red in the face. She screwed her eyes up. She looked as if she was trying hard not to cry. But Ruby never cries.

'Ruby,' I said, and I put my arm round her.

She wriggled away as if my arm had turned into a snake.

'Oh, Ruby,' I said, and I was the one who started crying. 'Look, I'm not going to go to Marnock Heights. I didn't even want to go in the first place. It was you that wanted to, not me.'

I was making it worse.

'I think you should go, Garnet,' said Rose. 'You've done very well. We should all be busy congratulating you. I know it's tough on Ruby, but—'

'You don't know anything,' I shouted.

I couldn't stand it. I didn't want them ganging up on my side. I was on Ruby's side.

'Hey, we'll have less of that cheeky tone,' said Dad. 'Rose, love, could you make us all a cup of coffee? Let's talk it over, eh? It's been a bit of a shock for all of us. Ruby? Ruby, where are you going?'

'There's nothing to talk about,' said Ruby. Her voice sounded awful. She was trying to make it sound couldn't-care-less, but it kept catching in her throat. 'Garnet's got the scholarship. I haven't . And that's it.'

'But I'm not going, Ruby! Please believe me. I promise I'm not going to go. I couldn't stand going there. Especially without you.'

'So why did you try ever so hard in all those silly tests and write all that yucky stuff for your essay?' said Ruby.

'I don't know. I just didn't think. Oh, Ruby, I'm sorry.'

I tried to grab hold of her again but she wouldn't let me.

'You get away from me,' she said, ducking.

'Now this is getting ridiculous,' said Dad. 'Pull yourself together, Ruby. I'm ashamed of you. I know you've had a bit of a disappointment, but there's no need to be nasty to poor old Garnet. Why can't you be big enough to congratulate her? She didn't act like this over that television audition, now did she? She was full of praise for you.'

Dad was making it worse. I saw Ruby's eyes, as she ducked. They were brimming over.

'Oh, congratulations, clever goody-goody Garnet,' Ruby gabbled, and then she rushed out the room.

I tried to follow her, but Dad stopped me.

'No, Garnet. Let her go. She won't want you around for a bit, especially as she's crying,' he said. Perhaps he did understand a little bit after all. 'But there's no need for you to cry, sweetheart. Rose is right. You've done brilliantly and I'm very proud of you.'

'I'm not going though,' I wept.

'Well. I can't make you go. And this boarding school lark certainly wasn't my idea.'

But I do think now that it's a wonderful opportunity.'

'I'll say,' said Rose, handing round the coffee. 'You've got to go for it, Garnet.'

'I can't leave Ruby,' I wailed.

'But Ruby would leave you,' said Rose.

'That's different,' I said.

'But it shouldn't be different,' said Dad, and he pulled me on to his lap. 'This letter has made me see that maybe it's bad for you and Ruby to be together all the time. You're holding each other back, spoiling each other's chances. You're growing up now, and you need to develop as two separate sisters.'

'But we're not separate. We're twins. We can't do without each other.'

'You're going to have to learn to some day,' said Dad. 'You'll both grow up and have different jobs and have different lifestyles and have different families.'

'No, we're going to stay together,' I said.

We'd got it all sorted out.

We'd stick together when we were young

and when we were old

and when we were even older

and if we ever wanted to get married then we'd marry twins

and have twin babies

and then when they grew up they *could stick together for ever and maybe they'd have twins too and then* they *could . . .*

My head was buzzing with all these twins. I wanted my own twin. I could hear her upstairs. She was sobbing.

I don't know what to do.

It's worse than when Ruby wasn't talking to me.

She's talking now, but not *properly*. And she only talks when we're with other people. When we're together she hardly says anything. She won't play any of our games. She won't plan any twin-tricks so that we do things simultaneously.

She doesn't seem to want to be a twin any more.

She won't even dress like me now. She waits until she sees what I'm putting on and then she puts on something entirely different. And she does her hair in a new way too.

I tried to copy her, so she changed it again.

And so I changed too. And then she did something terrible. She got the scissors and I thought she was bluffing. And then I wasn't sure.

'Don't!' I said.

But she did. She cut off all her hair.

'Oh Ruby, what have you done?' I said, looking at her poor head with the chopped hair sticking up like a scrubbing brush.

'I'm making me different,' she said, running

her hand through the stubble. She swallowed and sniffed. 'And you needn't look like that. I like it. I wanted it this way for ages. It's . . . sort of punk. Great.'

I didn't know what to do. We've always had long hair, right from when we were little. When Gran made us have plaits I would always do Ruby's as well as my own. Sometimes when I was feeling sleepy I'd forget which was my head and which was hers.

Now when I stared at Ruby I felt as if my own hair had been hacked off even though I could still feel the warm weight of it on my shoulders. It gave me the weirdest out-of-synch feeling, like when you watch a film and the people say things a fraction before their lips open.

Ruby couldn't grow her hair. So there was only one thing to do.

'No you don't!' Ruby hissed, as I reached for the scissors. She snatched them away from me. 'I'm warning you, Garnet. You cut off your hair and I'll cut off your head!'

She looked so fierce I felt I believed her.

She looked like she hated me.

She took the scissors and some newspaper and cut out a line of paper dolls. She cut them into twins. And then she chopped through their hands, so they were separate.

She chopped so violently that they tore all the way up their arms.

It's me again. Ruby won't write in the book any more. I don't want to write much either. How can I give an account of us when we aren't us any more.

If only I could tear out all the pages about the school and the scholarship – scrub them out so that they never happened.

Ruby's acting like she wants to scrub me out altogether. It's the holidays now, but she won't go around with me. She just goes off by herself and when I try to follow her she runs away. She could always run faster than me. And she's better at hiding. I don't know where she goes or whether she joins up with anyone else. But she won't join up with me.

I asked her in bed at night if we could go back to being us if I wrote a letter to Miss Jeffreys saying I wasn't going to Marnock Heights.

I waited. The room was very dark but I could see her eyes open, watching me. She waited too.

Then she said into the silence, 'I don't care if you go or not, Garnet. You do what you like. And I'll do what I like. But we're not us any more and we can't ever be. We'll still be split up even if we stay together.'

But it's not what I like. I don't know what I like.

I don't want to go to Marnock Heights. Although I've been reading all these books. Not the twins ones. I feel sick whenever I see them. No, there's a whole shelf of old school stories at the back of the shop – girls who go to schools in Abbeys and Chalets and Towers – and I've been reading one in the morning and one in the afternoon and sometimes one in the evening too and sometimes – just sometimes – it sounds as if it might be fun.

Judy thinks so. She's dead envious. She comes round to the shop sometimes. I've been to tea at her house. She's got all these tapes and videos. You just have to sit and watch and listen. Or we go up to her bedroom and play games. Not our sort of games. Board games. And I do get a bit bored playing them. Judy's OK but she's a bit boring too.

She says she's seen Ruby going around with Jeremy Treadgold and his gang! Ruby with the Giant Blob??? I asked Ruby but she just rubbed the end of her nose, indicating that I should mind my own business.

Ruby doesn't want to be my business any more.

She's made herself different.

She even looks different.

People maybe wouldn't even think we were twins now.

Gran nearly did her nut when she came to stay for the weekend. This old man, Albert, drove her in his car. He's her neighbour in her sheltered flats. He came and stayed too, which made it a bit of a squash. Gran said we should call him Uncle Albert, though he's not our uncle.

I looked at Ruby and she looked at me and just for a second it was almost like the old days.

But these are new days and everything's changing and Ruby's changed most of all.

'WhatEVER have you done to yourself, Ruby???' Gran demanded. 'What DO you look like? You're such a scruff. Like a gutter child. And your HAIR! Oh my lord, have you got nits?'

'Leave off, Gran,' said Ruby, fidgeting and scowling.

'For goodness sake, how could you let her run round like a ragamuffin?' Gran said to Rose.

Rose had tried to smarten Ruby up a bit for Gran's visit. She'd washed all her best clothes and ironed them and she'd begged Ruby to let her try to neaten up her new hairstyle. Ruby refused. She wore her oldest dirtiest clothes and deliberately fished her old holey trainers out of the dustbin, even though Rose had bought her brand-new ones specially.

But Rose didn't say any of this.

'Ruby likes to be comfy. And we think her hairstyle really suits her, don't we, Ricky?'

'Sure,' said Dad, putting his arm round Rose.

'Well, at least Garnet looks fairly presentable,' Gran sniffed. 'But what's all this I hear about you being packed off to boarding school, Garnet? I don't hold with that idea at all. What's the matter, do they want to get rid of you?'

'Of course we don't want to get rid of her!' said Dad. 'We just think she should give it a try for a term, seeing as she's got this scholarship. But if she hates it then of course she can come home whenever she wants.'

But like I said, I still don't know what I want. I'm starting to get nightmares about going to the school.

And yet it's horrid at home now that Ruby is a stranger instead of a sister. I'd secretly hoped that I could talk to Gran in secret and ask her if I could maybe go and live with her for a bit – but I'd forgotten how naggy and niggly she can be sometimes. And then there's Albert who isn't our uncle. He's not part of our family but it looks as if he and Gran are a new family all of their own.

Then there's Dad and Rose. They have rows sometimes but they always make it up and when Rose tried ever so hard to cook a proper Sunday lunch for everyone, but somehow the beef got burnt and the Yorkshire pudding sulked and the potatoes wouldn't roast and

the beans went stringy and the gravy had
lumps, Dad still ate up every scrap on his

plate and said it was super and even asked for
seconds.
    They're a family too.

*I'm part of their family and Gran's family
and I used to have Mum as special family but
even more than Mum there was always Ruby.*
Ruby-and-Garnet.
Only now there's just Ruby. And Garnet.

Ruby?

Ruby.

Oh, Ruby.

THIRTEEN

This is my written work. And I don't give a toss if it's slapdash. Who cares what that stupid jumped-up jelly-belly Jeffreys says?

I wouldn't want to go there anyway. Not now. I'm having heaps better fun here. I am.

Anyway, I bet Garnet doesn't have the bottle to go without me.

Or if she does, I bet she gets terribly homesick and cries heaps and will be sent back a sodden wreck.

She can't manage without me. Even she knows that.

But I'm doing just fine without her.

This is my new notebook and I shall take heaps of notes. It says MEMORANDUM on the cover. I like the first two letters. ME ME ME ME ME ME ME ME ME ME ME ME ME ME ME ME ME.

This notebook is going to be all about Me.

I like being just me.

I like it just me. Oh, I've put that bit
before. Never mind. It makes it twice as true.
I feel GREAT.

I know what Memorandum means, too. I am quite intelligent actually, even if some people seem to think I'm a total thicko. Memorandum means notes of things to be remembered. And I want it officially down on paper that

1. Ruby Barker doesn't give two hoots about not getting that stupid scholarship.

2. Ruby Barker doesn't give two hoots that her sneaky sister is going instead of her.

3. Ruby Barker doesn't give two hoots about said sneaky sister.

She is *absolutely devastated* (there, *I'm* the one who uses ever such posh long grown-up words, so it just goes to show that Miss Jeffreys is talking RUBBISH).

Yuck! Now. Where was I?

Oh yes. Garnet is truly despairing because I have broken up our twinship. She needs me.

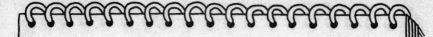

She might think she's the clever one now, but not a bit of it! She's utterly lost without me. But *I'm* fine. I don't need her. Not one *bit* of her.

Well, maybe her hand would come in useful some of the time. So she could do the writing when I get bored.

I do get a little bored sometimes. I go out because I don't want to stay in that smelly old shop, but there aren't many places to go to in this horrible dump. So I just sort of mooch about.

I don't need Garnet to make up games for me. I can make up my own. I mostly pretend I'm this intrepid explorer trekking through the jungle, and there are killer snakes and huge hairy poisonous spiders

and ferocious tigers

and I wade through the rapids

and hang by my fingertips from dangerous mountains

and whenever I get the merest glimpse of the enemy I have to hide because in spite of my superhuman powers and mega-brilliance I am hopelessly outnumbered.

I am planning an ambush when the Blob goes unprotected.

The Intrepid Explorer often starves for days and days. She has to make quick raids into enemy territory

but often has to make do with natural resources.

The Intrepid Explorer did ponder about doing a bit of hunting

but she decided she was a vegetarian. Even though she doesn't actually go a bundle on vegetables. Sprouts . . . yuck. Cabbage . . . yuck. Cauliflower . . . double yuck.

If this is a *Memorandum* book, then it's just about *me* . . . and I can jot things down at *randum*. I know what that means too, Miss Jeffreys, so ya boo sucks to you. It means there's no plan, and you just shove things in any old how. So these are my random jottings.

I am Ruby Barker and I am a brilliant actress and if my ex-twin hadn't made such a muck of things then I could be starring in a telly serial this summer.

I tried phoning the television people, telling them I was willing to audition for any other part. They thanked me and said they'd get in touch. But they didn't. So I phoned again and they got a bit shirtier this time and said there weren't any parts going spare, sorry and all that but would I quit pestering them please, and if I really wanted to be an actress I needed to get myself an agent and why didn't I go to a good stage school.

Well, how can I go to a good stage school when my rotten old father won't send me to one, though he's sending my sister to the poshest boarding school in the country.

OK, he doesn't have to pay fees, but her uniform is costing a *fortune*.

You should see it too. Talk about awful and old-fashioned! I wouldn't be seen *dead* in those clothes. Garnet looks *appalling*.

Well, I suppose Dad isn't having to pay out of his own pocket. Rose helped Garnet sell her doll at an auction. The crummy china baby doll, twin to mine. I sold mine at the car-boot sale and they gave me £20.

It is exceedingly painful to have to write this next bit. Garnet's doll went for £600. Yes. Mine would have been worth that too. It's some rare French make and daft doll-collectors are willing to fork out a fortune. I mean, you could probably buy a real baby for that sort of money.

Rose was very very angry when she found out the car-boot people only gave me £20. Not angry with me, with them. She went and found them and kicked up a great fuss, but they argued that it had been a perfectly fair deal and she was in the business and she should know they weren't running a kiddie's charity. But they did very reluctantly hand over £100. As a gesture. Rose was still cross because she said they must have made heaps more, but I was happy because that £100 is mine, and although boring old Dad said I should put it in a building society, Rose said she didn't see why I shouldn't have some spending money as I was having a bit of a tough time just lately.

Only I'm not having a tough time at all. Like I said, I'm fine. Doing great. Couldn't be better. *And* I've ended up with £50 to spend all on ME (plus £50 in Dad's boring old building society).

I don't have to waste it on a horrid, hideous

school uniform either. And special suitcases and hockey sticks and dressing gowns and frightful Clarks clodhopper shoes.

I can spend it on

or

or

or

or

or

or

It's weird. I've never had my very own money to spend before. I've always had to share. So it's great to get twice as much.

It's just I can't quite get used to being just me.

I don't even look like me. It's a shock whenever I see myself in the mirror. My hair's growing a bit but it seems to have lost all idea of gravity. It's growing *up*.

This has attracted comments from certain uncouth local loonies, enquiring whether I'm a boy or a girl.

I soon dealt with them.

But then the Huge and Horrible Blob opened his horrendous gob.

He had *such* an inventive and witty new nickname for me.

So I invented several new names for him and his stupid mates.

So then they got all these grass cuttings
and asked me if I'd like a green wig and then
they threw them all over me

so I hid behind a hedge until I heard them
coming and then I jumped up and yelled that
they all talked a lot of rubbish so look out—

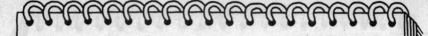

and they got this black plastic bag full of
rubbish all over them.

I'd just grabbed a bag out of someone's
dustbin. I hadn't looked inside. It turned out
it was wondrously smelly soggy rubbish, all
sour milk and tea-leaves and half-eaten
Chinese takeaways . . .

So then they got really mad and
yelled, 'Let's get her!'

I couldn't run away quite fast enough.

So they got me.

And they smeared rubbish on me and I hit
out at them and they kicked me and I bit
them but there was only one of me and there
were a lot of them.

And then while Blob and I were bashing away at each other, this horrible boy with ferret teeth got his arm round my neck and started choking me and I tried to reach round and hit him where it really hurts but he was hurting that wobbly bit where you swallow so much that I couldn't move and Ferret-Face yelled, 'Go on then, Jerry, bash her face in!' and I thought, This is it. I've already lost my hair. Now I'm going to lose my looks. I'm going to have to go round with a broken nose and no teeth for the rest of my days, and it's not going to help my acting career one bit, and I had my face all squeezed up ready for the blow but Blob hesitated.

'Leave go of her, Brian, she's choking,' he said.

'Well, hit her then!'

'Not with you hanging on to her. And all you others. It's not fair. We'll just fight it out, her and me.'

Ferret-Face muttered and moaned, but he did leave go. I reeled a bit, rubbing my sore neck.

'Are you OK?' said Blob.

'Course I am,' I croaked.

'Right. Let's fight,' said Blob.

So he gave me a punch on the shoulder. Quite a soft punch. And I gave him a shove in

his stomach. But not too hard. And then he
wrestled me to the ground. But carefully. And
I kicked at him. Though I actually barely
touched him. We seemed to have lost interest
in a really ferocious fight. We were just sort of
going through the motions.

Ferret-Face and the other mates got a bit
bored with the whole situation too. And they
were fed up being covered in all the stinky
guck from the rubbish bag, so they sloped off
home.

Blob and I were left.

'Shall we just say that I've won the fight and call it quits?' said Blob.

'You haven't won the rotten fight!' I said indignantly. I gave him another punch, though it was a very feeble one.

'All right all right. Well, how about if we call it a draw?' said Blob.

I thought a bit. And then I nodded.

'OK. Though I could have won, you know,' I insisted.

'You're quite a good fighter. For a girl,' said Blob.

'You're quite a good fighter. For a big fat blob,' I said.

He looked hurt. 'Hey, there's no need to call me names. I stuck up for you! I stopped Brian mangling your neck.'

'Yes, but you call me names. Baldie.'

'Yes, well, you do look a bit bald since you had that wacky haircut.'

'Yes, well, you do look a bit blobby.'

'We *both* look a right sight. Especially now. Covered in all this gunge,' said Blob, wiping bamboo shoots out of his eye.

'You can say that again,' I agreed, picking tea-leaves off my face.

We looked at each other. Then we laughed. And it's weird. We're not bitter enemies any more. We're sort of friends.

I sometimes go round in the gang, though I can't stick Brian. Actually, Blob isn't too keen on him either.

So we've started going round together. Just him and me.

He still calls me Baldie.

I still call him Blob.

But it doesn't matter because we're mates.

It's great to have someone to pal round with. Someone different, not someone the same as me.

And both Blob and I are going on to the big school together. I'm glad I'll be shot of that Dumbo Debenham. I'll be a new girl at a new school with new teachers. I could make a whole new start if I wanted. Work a bit.

Well, that's what Dad says.

I'll have to see about that.

But there is one good thing about the new school. They've got a stage. Not quite as posh and elaborate as the one at Marnock Heights, but they've got velvet curtains, and they can put up special lights and rustle up some scenery and they have a proper play in the summer and a pantomime at Christmas. Blob told me, because his sister's been in them.

So I'm going to get to be in them too.

Definitely.

It's all going to be great.

I'm ever so happy.

Garnet isn't happy. She's started crying at nights. She's scared about going to boarding school by herself. But it's not just that. She says she can't bear not being friends with me any more.

I listen. And sometimes my eyes sting a bit, but it's OK in the dark. She can't see.

I open my mouth to say a whole lot of
things. But somehow I can't ever get them
said into the silence. I can't even manage one
word. Sorry.

Well, I don't see why I should say sorry. It's
Garnet's fault she's going. She shouldn't have
done so well in that stupid entrance exam.

No, she should have tried harder at the
audition. Then we'd have got to be the Twins
at St Clare's. We'd be acting now. Together.

We've been separate all summer.

It's been a bit strange sometimes.

It's going to be even stranger when she's
gone.

It's her last night at home. Rose cooked
chicken and chips, Garnet's favourite, and
made a cake.

180

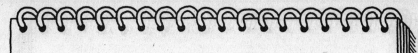

She's never made *me* a special cake.
Garnet could only manage one small slice.
Then we all had to sit around playing daft games like Snap and Happy Families. Pretending we were all one Happy Family. And Garnet looked like she was going to snap.

But she didn't cry. Not even when we went to bed. At least, I don't think she did. I got right under the covers so that I couldn't hear.
I felt as if I was snapping. In half.
I kept pretending it wasn't really happening but then we woke up in the morning and Garnet got dressed in her strange new uniform and we've never looked less like twins in our lives.

Rose came into our bedroom to help Garnet get all her new stuff packed and ready.

I looked at all the new clothes and the pyjamas and the hockey boots and all the other stuff, all exactly my size. But not for me.

And for the first time I was really glad I wasn't going. I knew I'd be scared.

Garnet was so scared she had a funny tummy and had to keep dashing to the loo. One of the times she was missing in the bathroom I picked up her old nightie lying on her pillow and sort of snuggled into it for a second, like a baby with a cuddle blanket.

Rose was bent over Garnet's suitcase but she turned and saw me.

She didn't say anything – but she straightened up and put her arm round me and gave me a quick hug.

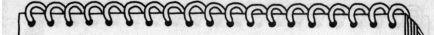

I started to wriggle away, but she held on to me. So I found I was kind of hugging her back.

And then I started crying.

'You're the one that never cries. You'll start me off,' Rose whispered.

'Don't be nice to me. I've been so hateful. To Garnet,' I sobbed.

'You haven't been exactly sweetness and light to me, either,' said Rose, laughing shakily. 'Or your dad. But you're right. It's Garnet that really matters.'

It's Garnet that really matters.

My twin. My best friend. My other half.

She came back from the bathroom and I rushed at her, flinging my arms round her neck.

'Oh Garnet, I'm so sorry, I've been such a pig, I didn't mean it really, I was just so jealous, and I felt so stupid, and I felt so left out, but you will still be my twin, won't you, even though you're off to Marnock Heights?'

'I'll be your twin for ever and ever and ever,' said Garnet, and we hugged so hard we seemed like Siamese twins, joined for ever.

Only we were about to be ripped apart.

'It's all my stupid stupid stupid fault,' I wailed. 'Oh Garnet, I'll miss you so terribly.'

'I'll miss you too, Ruby – ever so ever so much. But Dad says I don't have to stay if I really hate it.'

'And you'll come home some weekends – and all the holidays. Oh, how can I have been crazy enough to waste all this summer being so foul? I hate me. Why do I always have to be the bad twin?'

'Why do I always have to be the good twin?' said Garnet. 'Hey, maybe we're changing round. We're starting already. You're crying – and I'm not!'

'You will still be my best friend, won't you? You won't go all posh and snooty and look down on me?' I said.

'Don't talk wet,' said Garnet.

'And you will write to me?'

'Every single day. And you write to me too.'

'I promise.'

'You don't always keep your promises.'

'But this is a promise I'll keep, I swear. And I also promise that I'll never ever be mean to you again, Garnet.'

'You'd better not swear on *that* promise,' said Garnet, laughing.

But she cried a little bit when she and Dad went off in the car. We *all* cried.

Garnet's taken the accounts book with her. She's going to write in it every day and then show it to me when she comes home. I've nearly finished this memorandum book already.

I'll have to get another. Bigger, so I can write more. I'll look and see if there's a Paperchase in Hineford on Saturday. Rose is going to drive me there. She's found out about this Saturday drama club. So I'm joining it.

I was dead chuffed when she told me about it.

'Thanks, Rose,' I said.

Well. It was more of a mumble. But she heard.

'It's OK, Ruby. I'm dying to go to Hineford to see some decent shops. I'll have a lovely time in the shopping centre while you do your drama session and then we'll meet up and have lunch. Yes?'

'You bet,' I said.

She's not quite so bad as I thought, Rose.

It's time I started some serious drama training. For my big moment when the telly people get in touch and ask me to audition. Because they still *might*. If this *Twitty Twins at St Clare's* serial is a success they might want to do another Enid Blyton book. One of the Famous Five stories, maybe. The leading part is this fierce tomboy girl, Georgina. I could play her easy-peasy. I've even got the right haircut now.

When Dad gives me a big cuddle, he ruffles all the bristles and calls me his little

Scrubbing Brush. Dad's needed quite a lot of cuddles. Because he's missing Garnet so much.

We're all missing her.

I'm missing her most.

But she's all right. She sort of likes it.

I'll stick her first postcard on this page.

> Dearest Ruby,
>   I'm here! At Marnock Heights.
> I feel just like one of the girls in those
> old school books. I cried a bit after Dad
> left but this lovely big girl put her
> arm round me. She's called Jamilla
> and she's my Sheepdog. That doesn't
> mean she barks at me, she just shows
> me where everything is, the classrooms
> and my bedroom and the dining-room.
> We had chicken and chips for supper.
> And Jamilla gave me half a Kit Kat.
> I'm in the bedroom now and there are
> three other girls and we're all setting
> our alarms for midnight so we can
> have our first feast! The girl in the
> bed next to me is called Lucy, and
> she wears little glasses and she's got
> a toy rabbit to take to bed and a real
> rabbit in the zoo and she says I can
> share it if I want. She wants to be
> my best friend and I said yes but
> you're my _bestest_ best friend, Ruby. xxx
>   With lots and lots of love from Garnet xxxx
>   P.S. I do miss you so.

Oh, Garnet. I miss you too. Ever so ever so much.

But we're still Ruby and Garnet, even though you're there and I'm here.

We're going to be Ruby and Garnet for ever.

THE END